Dedication

Out of the Zone is dedicated to
the 1961 graduating class
of Oak Park-River Forest High School,
in honor of celebrating
fifty years of a remarkable adventure.

Acknowledgments

I spent the past two summers writing in a 104-year-old farm cottage located in Sequim, Washington. Although the serene setting offered an idyllic place to write, it had no Internet connection. To retrieve my e-mails and interact with people, I'd drive into town and spend hours at the Hurricane Coffee Company. Teresa, the owner, and Sandy, the manager, welcomed me with a smile and permitted me to plug in my computer, spend the day in a remote corner and work with endless cups of freshly brewed coffee. Thank you for providing me with a sanctuary to write. You made my creative process cheerful and inviting.

In November, 2009, the 1961 reunion committee purchased a website program from Class Creator, a company that specializes in providing such a service for organizations like ours. The program permitted members of our class to share personal information, to contribute favorite memories about school life, and to chat about recollections of Oak Park-River Forest High School and the village we called home. I read profiles as they were posted on the site, and the information not only provided interesting insights about former classmates, but also motivated me to write this novella. I want to thank the members of the committee for their efforts to connect all of us together as a class again and to turn the reunion into a special celebration. Members of the 1961 Class Reunion Committee include: Dick Carey, Cille (Sorrentino) Bucolo, Tom Weyburn, Joyce (Conlon) Dunn,

Kyle Westerman, Cathy (Spellmire) Schreiner, Bonnie McKirnan, George Schultz, Doug Sainsbury, Maggie (Schulz) Tafilaw, Holly (Hitchcock) Wilson, Bill Meyers, Bob Bristol, Jody (Cavanaugh) Newman, George Wohlford, Les Golden, Chuck Andersen and Nancy (Leabhard) Strand. This event would not have happened without your tireless efforts.

Karen Parris, my proof editor, continues to be my North Star. Her editing skills provide guidance and security to my adventures in storytelling. Like the seafarers of olden day, I look to Karen to safely guide my novel across an ocean of ever-changing Chicago-style rules and the most current writing expectations. I may have the courage to unfurl the sails and tack into the winds of the unknown, but Karen always keeps the ship on course and moving in its intended direction. Thank you for making a sailor out of me and preventing my novels from sinking.

Rebecca Reynolds, Rosel Sersante and Donna Morey continue to volunteer as my first-draft manuscript readers. As Ernest Hemingway once said, "The first draft of anything is shit." In spite of the rough slogging through my first drafts, these three ladies put on their hip waders, read through each chapter and gave me sweet words of encouragement that turn my initial odoriferous drafts into an aromatic experience. Thank you for offering this novice writer your gentle gifts of encouragement. A special thanks also goes to Carol Hinrichs (Stickling) who used to let me copy her notes in English class fifty years ago. Recently, she agreed to read the final proof of this story to make sure I incorporated some of her ideas.

Disclaimer

This book recounts an imaginary story, and all characters and dialogue are purely fictional. Some of the ideas for the events portrayed in the novel were gleaned from profiles posted on the 1961 class reunion website. Others form discussions with people who lived, loved, laughed and met the various challenges that come with life.

However, any resemblance to individuals portrayed in the story, living or dead, is purely coincidental. Some of the settings may seem familiar to the reader, and the author has blended various locations to create a generic image of the fictitious town of Oak Ridge, Illinois. Perhaps these places and personal stories will evoke fond memories of your own high school experience and motivate you to share them with friends and family.

The quotes at the beginning of each chapter are intended to set the tone for the action that follows. Although all of the people are real, none of them attended the high school.

Mark Pierce, a purely fictional character, never attended or graduated from Oak Ridge High School in 1961, but he could have. His name symbolically represents "an unwanted guest who left a memory of his presence."

Initial Reflection

In 1961, Oak Park and River Forest graduates (Oak Ridge) entered adult life with a spirit of optimism. Over the next five decades, each of them made significant life decisions. One possible decision could have kept them in a comfort zone created by the sedate, familiar culture of Oak Park, Illinois. The other choice may have lured them away, out of the zone, to experience a life filled with questions and unknown adventures. Robert Frost eloquently spoke to such a dilemma. He challenged us to think about the conundrum of making choices that may send us in a direction that will be impossible to change in later years.

Excerpts from
"The Road Not Taken"
by Robert Frost

Two roads diverged in a yellow wood,
And sorry I could not travel both …

… Yet knowing how way leads on to way,
I doubted if I should ever come back.

I shall be telling this with a sigh
Somewhere ages and ages hence:
Two roads diverged in a wood, and I —
I took the one less traveled by,
And that has made all the difference.

A Stretch of the Imagination

Imagine if you will that Ernest Hemingway graduated with us in 1961. Impossible, you say! Just for a moment, I ask the reader to suspend disbelief and accept this premise. What if Hemingway had been one of our classmates? How would his knowledge and life experiences contribute to our collective wisdom?

In real time, Ernest Hemingway graduated from Oak Park-River Forest High School in 1917. Like most of us, Hemingway was neither a brilliant student, nor an outstanding athlete. In high school, he struggled with grades and earned a "D" in an English class. Hemingway participated on the football team, tried swimming, played water basketball and served as a manager on the track team. He submitted humorous articles to the school's newspaper, the *Trapeze*. His social life in high school remains a mystery, but like most adolescents, he was probably awkward and unaware of the social graces required for success with the opposite sex. Sounds like most of us, doesn't he?

Born in a house at 339 N. Oak Park Avenue, Hemingway went through the Oak Park school system and grew up in a conservative, Protestant, all-white culture. Several sources suggest that he later referred to his hometown as "a place of wide lawns and narrow minds." However, the truth of that quote has never been verified. He chose to leave the familiar tranquility of Oak Park and discover other aspects of life.

After graduating high school, his uncle got him a job as a cub reporter for *The Kansas City Star*.

From these humble, ordinary beginnings, Hemingway embraced life with enthusiasm. He desired to live on the edge to experience life in its most raw form. From serving as an ambulance driver in Italy during World War I to his life as an expatriate in Paris, Hemingway witnessed significant historical events that had a profound effect on his writing. He embraced bizarre encounters and absorbed their emotional impact. His words, captured in the dialogue and passion of characters and stories, provide us with memorable impressions of our own humanity.

Given these experiences, what insights or advice would an older Hemingway classmate offer the 1961 graduates? The author of this novel has taken the liberty to sort through his more famous lines and included some of them for your reflection as if this famous "classmate" were an interested observer. They appear in bold at the end of each chapter and serve as his commentary on the action taking place. For example: His thoughts on this novel,

> **"All good books have one thing in common — they are truer than if they had really happened."**
> **— Ernest Hemingway**

Chapter One:
The Invitation

"Never look back unless you are planning to go that way."
— Henry David Thoreau

"How the hell did they find me?" I shouted at a nonresponsive mailbox. *It's been fifty years since I graduated from high school, and now they've invited me to attend the class reunion.* "This is lunacy. I can't do that."

"Hey, Mark, what's going on? You upset about something?" said my neighbor.

Frank lives next door and broke his daily routine by waddling across my lawn in his fluffy bedroom slippers and tattered bathrobe to talk. Frank usually didn't function until an hour after downing three cups of coffee. Today, however, my outburst attracted his attention.

"I received an unexpected letter, that's all, Frank."

"I hope it's not bad news. Anything I can do to help?"

"No, it's not that important. I'll handle it. Thanks."

I held the letter to my chest with one hand and unconsciously touched the scars on my throat with the other. The letter had transformed my mood, and now Frank's curiosity irritated me. I apologized to him and turned to go back inside.

Before entering, I stopped and became reflective about the choices I had made in life. I loved living in the Bay Area with Linda — in this place and at this time, but what if things had been different? I had no desire to go back there and dredge up the past. For fifty years, I successfully suppressed uncomfortable, ancient memories, and now I'm being asked to attend a party to revive them.

I like my current lifestyle, and Linda has been a godsend. I owe my present tranquility to her. I looked around my yard and inhaled a contented breath. The recent rains had transformed the winter groundcover into a soft, green carpet, and the scent of new grass filled me with satisfaction. My mind jumped, and I made a mental note to repair the lawnmower.

I turned to watch the morning sun peek through the maple tree that adorned the front yard, casting playful designs on the grass. A refreshing breeze from the Pacific Ocean let me know another season had changed without fanfare. *April, one of my favorite months,* I thought, and then like a dark cloud, the letter jumped back into my head. *Why do I need to connect with anything or anyone from the good old days? They weren't that good for me.*

After commencement, I left Oak Ridge High School and never looked back. I embraced an intense wanderlust, motivated by the need to escape. I filled my backpack with basic survival essentials, laced my sleeping bag to its frame, and purchased an overseas airline ticket with the cash gifts I received from relatives at graduation. The next sixteen weeks offered an exploration of remote places in Europe — free and independent, released from parental control and those unmanageable events that sent me packing.

Liberated from a past peppered with youthful indiscretions, I learned how to survive in the real world. Shortly after I graduated from high school, my parents moved to Florida. For the next fifty years, neither friends, nor memories motivated me to return to Oak Ridge. I closed the book on that part of my life. I thought it was forever, until today.

I recall being the typical high school student. We all had similar behaviors, goals and aspirations. That changed at the end of my senior year and distanced me from my peers. Even though several class reunion invitations reached me over the years, I never attended any of those parties. I declined for legitimate reasons: job responsibilities, too busy, traveling — excuses piled up, and time passed without notice. Now after fifty years, a virtual stranger to my classmates, why would I bother to attend the fiftieth reunion?

I walked into the house still thinking about the letter I carried. The look on my face must have startled Linda. I'd been living with her for more than a decade, and she enjoyed an uncanny ability to accurately sense my every mood. She looked up from her computer and asked, "What's wrong, Mark? You look ghastly."

Linda rose and lovingly stroked my face. Her touch always melted my temperamental moods. She patiently waited for a response. Sensing Linda's anxiety, I managed a smile. "Oh, nothing, nothing," I grinned. *This woman loves me*, I thought. *I have to tell her.* "My past just invaded my present, and I have to decide if I want to embrace it."

Linda stroked the back of my neck and kissed me on the cheek. "What are you talking about?"

I showed her the invitation. She read it, chuckled and, in her typical way, hit me on the shoulder. "God, Mark, it's not like you got a letter from an IRS agent. Why such a morbid look?"

"Remember, right after graduation, I split town. Had I stayed in Oak Ridge, my life would have been devoured by a vortex — a dark hole of angry judgment. I didn't want to spend the rest of my life being the town's scapegoat."

Linda released an uncontrolled laugh and hit me on the shoulder again. She snickered, "You're such a drama queen, aren't you? That was fifty years ago. You make such a big deal out of running away — your great escape, as you call it. It's as if this invitation represents a living creature who wants to consume you."

I grimaced at her words and, slightly embarrassed, looked sheepishly at the envelope in my hand.

"When you walked in, I thought some friend or relative had died, or you were about to reveal the sordid details of a midlife crisis."

"You don't understand, Linda," I pleaded. "The decision to leave that little box I used to call my hometown was pretty traumatic for a seventeen-year-old kid."

"Yes, but you made the choice to leave, and everything after that evolved into better decisions — decisions that guided your future. You're not the same person you were as a teenager. You can't relive history, so stay in the present and enjoy the moment."

"Call me an old fool, but I still carry around a lot of anger about making that decision."

"I know you're an old fool," she teased, "but I have no idea why you're angry. You've refused to talk about that part of your life."

"It's difficult to explain, and I still don't want to talk about it now."

"I promise I won't make fun of you," she said. "Tell me what's really bothering you."

"I can't put my finger on it, but the older I get the more angst I have felt about the decisions I made back then. I ask myself, 'What if I had stayed in Oak Ridge, worked out that crap and made a life there instead of running away? How would it have been different? Would I have been happier than I am now?'"

"Absolutely not. You wouldn't have met this beautiful woman standing in front of you," she smiled. "Look, Mark, why don't you tell me what happened so I can understand."

"No, Linda. That's a part of the past, and I will never talk about it. All you need to know is that I have always wondered about the *what if* question in life."

"I can assure you that's natural at your age. People often begin to have second thoughts about the choices they made. It goes with the aging territory."

"It's deeper than that with me," I said. "At times I'm upset for not having the courage to face my critics and the truth back then. I could have made something of myself in spite of the circumstances."

"No need to regret the past," she said. "For every step people take in one direction, the more options and experiences they leave behind. Sort of like Frost's poem."

"That's my point … I feel angry I took the road less traveled and that may have made a huge difference because I'm still on it."

"Aren't you happy now?"

"Yes, but …."

"But, what?"

"I don't know if I sacrificed happiness by leaving Oak Ridge like I did."

"Mark, I'm sure many of your classmates left Oak Ridge and found contentment along the way. Staying in the security of Oak Ridge didn't guarantee people would be happy."

"Perhaps you're right, but I'll never know."

"You could get a glimpse if you decide to go back and talk with your classmates about the decisions they made."

"Based on what happened, I'm not sure any of them will want to talk with me."

"Of course, they will," Linda lectured. "You're no longer a young kid, or think like one. You've explored your dreams, made a few big mistakes and recovered from life's challenges

— and so have your classmates. Nobody will hold you responsible for the *sins of the past*." Linda gave me a quick hug and looked into my eyes.

I stood motionless for several moments and thought about going back to Oak Ridge. *Is it possible they would remember and still be mad at me?* I wondered. *I'm different and so are they.*

Linda caught the grin breaking in the corners of my mouth and asked, "So, what's that clever mind of yours conjuring up, dear one?"

"Nothing spectacular. You're right. It may be an interesting adventure to step back in time. I think I could do this — and even enjoy a trip back to Oak Ridge. I've put it off way too long."

"Nothing like facing old demons and answering nagging questions about life. I'm proud of you," she said.

"Very true," I said. "However, I need to do this reunion thing by myself, so I'm not inviting you to accompany me."

"Good for you, my brave pathfinder. This is one of those singular, personal experiences only you can appreciate. Since I don't know any of those people, I'd be bored, anyway."

"I appreciate an independent woman like you instead of some of those clinging vines I used to date, who relied on me for their emotional support. I love you because you know how to take care of yourself."

"Exactly the way I like it, too," she said. "Besides, living with you provides me with all the entertainment I can handle. It's more than I ever anticipated." Giving me another quick kiss and a warm hug, she giggled, "You're sort of an unexpected bonus to my life, my own video game."

We both laughed.

"I'll be gone for four or five days. What will you do while I'm away?"

"That's easy. I'll take a few days off, grab the dog and go camping in the Sierras. You know how I love my alone time. The mountains will be absolutely gorgeous in September."

"Then, it's settled. This stranger will start planning to return to his long-lost land of mystery and reconnect with his former high school days."

"Cowardice ... is almost always
simply a lack of ability
to suspend functioning of the imagination."
— Ernest Hemingway

Chapter Two: Anticipation

"We can never know about the days to come
But we think about them anyway …
Anticipation, anticipation is makin' me late,
is keeping me waitin' …"
— Carly Simon

Although September was six months away, I began to have second thoughts about going back. Returning after fifty years scared me. I tried to prepare for the trip by pretending I had to make a voyage to some distant land. Oak Ridge must have changed, because I certainly had. *What should I take back as a personal "talking stick" to best define my life?*

I first thought a small picture album would do the trick. The old cliché "a picture is worth a thousand words" stuck in my mind, and I headed to the attic. I burrowed through dusty boxes and hauled down my old photos from the bygone days of Kodachrome-finished paper. I began humming Paul Simon's 1973 rendition of Kodachrome and then started singing it: "When I think back on all the crap I learned in high school …."

Linda heard me and walked into the kitchen warbling the next lines in her soprano voice, "It's a wonder I can think at all …." She stopped and giggled. "I didn't know you and Paul were friends in the seventies. The song describes you so well."

"Very funny." I spread the pictures on the kitchen table, and Linda joined me for a photographic journey into my dim past.

I looked at my image in the early prints and noticed how my face reflected youthful exuberance — filled with energy and ready to seek answers to all of life's most complicated questions. *What happened to that guy?* I pondered.

Linda examined the photos taken of me as I meandered through Europe. "I love these shots, dear. You can easily tell it's the sixties." I examined the pictures in her hand. Each print showed my hair growing longer, and I noticed my features subtly change as the wisdom of the experiences I encountered, good and bad, impacted my thinking.

"These snapshots look pretty dorky," I complained. "How much of this do I want to share?"

"Afraid they'll laugh at you?" Linda smiled. "All of us went through those awkward phases when time and fashion dictated styles. They'll understand because they were just like you."

I picked up a picture of a blonde with long, braided hair. *Beautiful Monika*, I thought. *Wow, what memories. Should I tell my classmates about meeting Monika and the lecherous month I spent in Eskilstuna, Sweden? I worked on her father's dairy farm by day and rolled in the hay with her at night. The little sweetheart transformed this boy into a man, and I will never forget her patience or her passion.*

"Who's that?" Linda asked.

"Just a Swedish girl who taught me some things about life." Linda wasn't amused by the tone of my response and socked me on my arm.

I discovered pictures of me bussing dishes on a Rhine River cruise and singing with my shipmates in a German tavern. The memory of drinking excessive amounts of dark beer conflicted with the sweetness of Peppermint Schnapps, and my stomach rebelled. Even to this day, I can't drink anything with a peppermint taste to it. *That's not important to share*, I thought.

"These pictures are interesting," said Linda, picking up another pile. "When were you in Greece?"

"I traveled on a train going through southern Italy and ran into a group of French guys headed to the Aegean. They planned to sail a ship owned by a family member, and invited me to join them on their nautical adventure. However, I don't remember much about the trip."

"Why? Did you fall overboard?"

"Nope, excessive amounts of Greek wine, complemented by an efficient hookah, made time and events slip away. But, I can see the pictures look like I had a good time."

"I'm glad I didn't know you back then."

"Not much to like. I was still searching."

"When did you discover a direction to take in life?"

"Not for quite a while. I drifted a lot."

As Linda sorted through the boxes, she noted a significant lack of pictures from my twenties. "What happened to those photos?" she asked.

"Those were the years I struggled with my identity and the disappointment of unmet dreams."

"Where are the pictures of your friends and family?" Linda asked.

"I spent plenty of alone time," I mumbled. "No Kodak moments worth capturing then. I did some cool things, but whenever they happened, nobody had a cell phone or camcorder to capture them for posterity. They weren't invented yet."

"Too bad you don't have any photographs of those days," she added.

"Yeah, but now there's no such thing as privacy. Someone's always pointing a digital device at you. Within minutes, your personal life flashes across the world on

Facebook or YouTube. I enjoy my private life and hate sharing my personal feelings about anything in the past."

"Then, taking these pictures to your reunion may not be such a good idea. You're a much better storyteller."

"Perhaps, I'll just stick with telling them about my career."

"Work's the easiest topic to share," Linda agreed.

"Ah, work — a safe, but superficial topic, and it can be explained without revealing too much." I paused and summarized my resume. "I'm into rocks ... received a B.A. in geology from the University of Colorado, and was hired by Standard Oil to find gas and oil deposits in remote places like Venezuela, Saudi Arabia, Alaskan Pipeline, offshore drilling platforms — nothing too significant, but each location offered its own adventures and entertainment."

"That's a good conversation starter," Linda added.

"Can I tell them about us, Linda?"

"I'd be upset if you didn't."

"I'll tell them how I was walking around the old Haight-Ashbury district and stepped into a used book store. Remember?"

"Of course, I do. I was there."

"I recall every delicious moment of our meeting," I said. "I stood in the bookstore, browsing for something to read, and spotted you. Sunbeams streamed through the window and bathed your face in a soft glow. You walked toward me with flashing green eyes and wispy brown hair. For a second, I couldn't breathe, and then words spilled out of your mouth. You said: 'Can I help you find something?' Do you remember how I answered, Linda?"

"Absolutely, so debonair ... such a suave pick-up line. You said I couldn't help you, because you had already found what you were looking for."

"Right, and then I immediately invited you to dinner. In reality, I just wanted to see how a bookstore owner felt between the covers."

"Bad pun, Mark," she groused and punched her favorite target on my arm, again. "I went out with you — overwhelmed by your self-aggrandizing charms. Even though the date burst my bubble, it started the beginning of this ten-year romance we've enjoyed," she said and hugged me.

"Linda, I don't think I have the words or the courage to share that kind of thing."

"Perhaps not," she cautioned, "especially if you tell our tale in your melodramatic fashion and end with your sexist comment."

"Okay, I'll only say you're my 'significant other' — the woman I live with, and we are co-owners of a funky, little bookstore in the Bay Area. That's enough."

A few pictures, some crazy travel stories ... enough to span five decades, I thought. *I'll gloss over personal events, and then I'll ask a lot of questions. That should be sufficient.*

"If you are lucky enough to have lived in Paris
as a young man, then wherever you go
for the rest of your life it stays with you,
for Paris is a moveable feast."
— Ernest Hemingway

Chapter Three:
The Intention

"Life takes on meaning when you become motivated, set goals and charge after them in an unstoppable manner."
— Les Brown

September would soon be the next month to appear on the wall calendar. The pleasant harvest pictured scared me. I now feared returning to the reunion because I didn't know how I'd come to grips with the event that sent me away. More importantly, what if I discovered I made a mistake by leaving town? *How would I resolve that?* My uneasiness turned to outright discomfort and, again, I contemplated not going. One night, Linda found me sitting in front of the fireplace, idly staring into the glowing embers, lost in distant thought.

She moved to the arm of my overstuffed chair, letting her fingers twirl the long strands of hair on my neck. "Okay, big guy, let's have it. Thinking about that reunion has isolated you from me, and I don't like it."

"Oh, I'm sorry. I didn't realize I had left you. It's that obvious?"

"Yes, I thought you had moved out, and I needed to advertise for a roommate," she giggled. I leaned into her warmth and reconnected with her body.

"I'm really sorry. I haven't thought about any of those people for such a long time. I have no idea what to expect."

"Don't let it throw you. I have an idea. Just approach it like you're a detective solving a mystery."

"That's silly. How can a reunion be like a detective story?" I asked.

"Whenever we talk about that time in your life, you clam up. It's all part of a foggy mystery to me. Sure, you did something weird," she said, making quote marks with her fingers, "but I have no clue why you continue to hide it from me."

"So, what's your point?" I asked.

"For me, it doesn't matter. You and I live in the present. Neither one of us has to live with the fallout from that clouded past."

"Yes," I said, "and that's the way I like it."

"But now they want you to come back and celebrate a milestone event. This may be your last opportunity to see most of your old classmates together and learn what happened to them. Find out for yourself if those who decided to stay in Oak Ridge are happier and more content than those, like you, who left."

"Yeah, I'm probably not the only one who broke the mold."

"What makes you think that those who stayed in Oak Ridge found a richer life than yours?"

"Don't know, but that would be interesting to discover."

"See," said Linda, "you don't have to worry about the reunion if you approach it like you're investigating a case."

"Right, kind of like a parlor game. My friend, John, did it in the kitchen with a candlestick."

"Get a clue," she laughed. "All of you are about sixty-seven or sixty-eight. No need for friends and acquaintances to pretend anymore. People have either made it — achieved their dreams — or they haven't."

"It would be interesting to see what choices they made."

"At your age, complete honesty will flow like a wide, quiet river, and they'll be happy to share — to have someone who will listen to their stories."

"It sounds like you're calling us old fogies."

"No, but people your age have lots of stories to tell. More importantly, people who used to be angry with you have been tempered by time and experience. How could anyone hold a fifty-year grudge? They'll be impressed that you are interested in them."

Linda's simple logic intrigued me. What impact did Oak Ridge High School have on people's lives and the choices they made after graduation? Did our time together make a difference? I jumped up and gave Linda a quick kiss and headed upstairs.

"What was that for?" she shouted after me.

"Just because you're brilliant, and I love you so much."

I returned with my Oak Ridge senior annual. I hadn't looked at it since May, 1961, and decades of accumulated dust had to be washed off before I could inspect it. I sat on the couch next to Linda, opened the front cover and turned the pages. We both laughed at the fashions, hairstyles and funny pictures. Then, we created a simple strategy for me to use when I returned to Oak Ridge.

When we got past most of the pictures that captured the school culture, Linda asked, "If you had a chance to spend four days with members of your graduating class — people you remembered most, who would you put on your short list?"

"Based on my history, not the popular ones — those voted 'most likely to succeed.' Perhaps I should go back to my elementary years and find those friends."

"Why don't you start with people you knew in your senior year?" Linda suggested.

"Okay," I responded, "how about I start with all the girls I wanted to date, the ones I dated and the ones I spent time with in my adolescent dreams?"

Linda frowned and landed another sharp blow to my left arm. "You're not going back to your reunion to hit on someone or rekindle a lost love, are you?"

"No, but that could be interesting."

"Not funny, bucko," she responded, tapping my arm again. "Make your list and walk into the reunion as an interested observer — there to learn tidbits about their personal stories. Some of your classmates have stayed in Oak Ridge all their lives. Find out if that made a difference. Others went away and have another kind of story to tell."

"That's it! I can be Mark, the life detective, mildly masquerading as a soft-spoken geologist — a former ghost from their past, now haunting their private party."

"God, Mark, why do you turn everything into a soap opera?"

"That's the only way I know how to deflect my feelings and have fun doing it. How do you suggest I get started?"

"Take me on a *who's who* tour of your senior year and tell me something about those you knew. A *must see* list will pop into your head. What do you think?"

"Excellent plan. Sure you won't get bored?"

"Fire away, Mark. Whatever you share will open all new vistas for me."

"Okay," I said, turning to the senior section of the annual. "Actually, this could be fun."

"However," Linda said, "please promise me you won't try any stupid detective impersonations."

"Me? None of that nonsense ever entered my mind," I smiled. "Just call me Jacques Clouseau, private eye. I can practice a little French vocabulary on you, *mon chéri.*"

She winced and took another swing at my embattled arm, but I intercepted her hand in mid-flight and kissed her knuckles. We grinned at each other and started the task.

"Let's see ... the first person is Kathy Abbott. I remember her as a quiet girl who spent a lot of time with her family in church. ... I don't know much else about her ... next ...."

Linda grabbed a notebook and pen and played recorder for me. We went through the seniors, and when I reached the last page, the list consisted of about twenty names.

"I don't know if I can talk with everyone on the list, but thanks. I feel better about the trip. Going back after fifty years seems rather daunting."

Over the next several weeks, Linda coached me through non-invasive ice breaker questions to ease my anxiety. My trepidation about the class reunion subsided, and I started marking off calendar days until the reunion. Linda thought I acted like a spoiled child, waiting to unwrap my Christmas presents.

Move over, Thomas Wolfe, I thought. *This man will be able to go home again.* But he will make the trip with the fresh eyes of curiosity — to discover how people I knew as an adolescent changed. *I wonder how many of their dreams and aspirations have been molded by fate or personal choice? God knows I've been haunted forever by the choice I made.*

"Perhaps as you went along
you did learn something. I did not care what it
was all about. All I wanted to know was how to
live in it. Maybe if you found out how to live in it
you learned from that what it was all about."
— Ernest Hemingway

Chapter Four:
An Insight

"Reality is merely an illusion, albeit a very persistent one."
— Albert Einstein

Shortly after Labor Day, Frank Montain called to personally invite me to the reunion and welcome me back to Oak Ridge. Frank and I went to elementary school together and shared the same tent on our Boy Scout outings. We ran for the cross-country team our freshman year, but an injury caused me to drop out of that sport. For the remainder of our high school career, Frank and I sat in some of the same classes and once doubled-dated to a dance. Back then, Frank could have been characterized as a friend, but I don't ever recall having a close pal in high school. I hadn't heard his voice in fifty years.

"Nice to talk with you again, Mark," Frank's effervescent voice seemed to shout into the phone.

"Yeah, nice to hear your voice, too, Frank," I offered in a subdued response.

"Just calling to confirm you're coming to the old reunion. Boy, do we have great things planned for this one."

The letter that accompanied the invitation indicated Frank had become sort of a local celebrity in Oak Ridge. He volunteered for the city as an event planner and now filled that role as the chairman of the Oak Ridge High School Alumni Association. The letter expressed his pride in organizing and hosting this special event.

"Yeah, I was surprised you guys found me. Thanks for the invitation. ... This time, I think I'll be able to make it."

Ignoring the uncomfortable silence that followed, his bubbly voice continued with a rehearsed speech.

"That's great, Mark. We located you through Standard Oil's early retirement list. You successfully avoided us by being out of the country on some long-term assignments when we scheduled the other reunions. We didn't know how the hell to contact you, old buddy. Don't you just love modern technology? Now you can't hide from anyone," he exuded a forced belly laugh.

In reality, they probably didn't want to contact me for any of those parties, I thought.

Frank's words sounded like a sales pitch for a used car commercial. His voice was smooth, inviting, and betrayed a tinge of patronization — a little too sweet and syrupy for my taste.

"With your name all over the reunion brochures, I guess you stuck around Oak Ridge and took charge of things," I commented.

"You bet, good buddy. I never went off to college. I began washing vehicles on my dad's car lot. Then, I moved into sales and took over for the old man after he retired. I'm proud to tell ya' I now run the biggest Chevrolet franchise in the county. If you lived closer, you'd see me on "Frank's Place," hot car commercials that air on local television five nights a week."

"My, my, Frank. You've put big wheels under that sleek body of yours, haven't you?" I said.

"Right you are, good buddy," he responded.

He didn't get it, I thought.

Completely disregarding my final days at Oak Ridge, Frank blustered about his success. I spotted his name on my *must see* list. He was one of the few guys that didn't send me hate mail when I couldn't attend classes during the last weeks of my senior year.

Frank seemed like a man who loved to talk about himself and would likely share meaningful insights without coaxing. This telephone conversation offered me an excellent opportunity to test some of the questions I planned to ask at the reunion.

"Wow," I said, "I thought a guy like you … with your ambition and talent — your drive … would have left old Oak Ridge and moved on to greener pastures, so to speak."

"No, no, not me, good buddy! The idea of leaving Oak Ridge never entered my mind. Tell you the truth, Mark, if you had stuck around instead of running off to parts unknown, you'd have figured out the secret of success happens right here with the people you know."

I almost gagged at his insolence and reference to my sudden departure, but stayed in character as "detective Mark" and nurtured his ego.

"I guess you're right, Frank. I missed the lifeboat that carried you to greatness."

I tried to tone down my disdain as much as I could, but I craved to belittle him for his bombastic assumptions and naive attitude. I remained pleasant. He continued, oblivious to the simplicity of his assumptions, and blathered on with unbridled enthusiasm. So, I decided to acquiesce and play my expected role in his mini-drama.

"The hell, you say!" Frank chortled into the phone. "Yup, my friend, I agree. You missed a lot of the good life here," he said, ignoring my dark past. Moving back into his "car-pitch mode," he added, "Haven't you always dreamed of living in a place, surrounded by a loving family to support your every move?"

He hesitated long enough to give me a chance to respond with an obligatory, "Yes."

"Have you ever wanted to own a piece of the American dream ... in an idyllic location where you feel comfortable and loved by friends and neighbors?"

He paused again so I could utter a second, "Yes."

"Have you ever thought about having a job that would provide you and your family with all your economic needs and wants?"

Again, he waited for another "yes" to roll off my tongue.

"Did you ever desire to feel safe, loved and respected by the community and know you are thriving in the loving arms of God?"

"Of course," I said, wincing in discomfort. His Oak Ridge sales pitch came unbearably close to the actual reason why I left town. I wanted to tell him to turn off his apostolic approach and stop marketing the joy of living in the comfort of our old hometown. I would have said that, but he paused only long enough to suck in a quick breath and continue. I realized I couldn't compete.

"Well, then, my friend, you passed up an opportunity to live in a little slice of heaven. Oak Ridge symbolizes the entrance to paradise, and it's too bad you didn't recognize it before you went away. You just up and left us too soon."

Not waiting for my response, he pressed his argument.

"Tell you what I'm going to do for you, good buddy. I'll set you up with one of our old classmates — Frazier Anderson. ... Remember him? He's a realtor with Re/Max and a close friend of mine. He'll be glad to work with you to find something in your price range. Owning a home in Oak Ridge will help overcome that lonely journey you've been on since departing our fair city fifty years ago. What do you say, buddy? Shall I have 'Fraz' contact you?"

To end his sermon and get him off my back, I lied, "Of course, Frank ..., why not?"

"Deal closed!" he shouted. "I'll let you go now ... just a courtesy call. ... Can't wait to see you again."

After Frank hung up, my anger flared. I debated things I should have said, but didn't. Then, it became clear to me. Frank had just defined the criteria for why people made their home in Oak Ridge and settle for the solace of that lifestyle. *What did it mean to live in a sanctuary like Oak Ridge instead of moving into the unknown?*

Excited, I called Linda into the den.

"I just talked with Frank Montain, the chairman of the reunion committee. He told me why we need to move back to Oak Ridge."

She dried her hands on a dishtowel and stared at me. "You've got to be kidding. You want us to move to Oak Ridge, Illinois?"

"No, no, not really, but I now know why people stayed there after high school and probably will remain there all of their lives." I took out my list and jotted down the reasons Frank shared: proximity to close friends, clean and safe community, good job, and spiritual guidance.

"Where are you going with this?" Linda asked. "Have you been brainwashed by a telemarketer?"

"Don't you see," I began, "it's not the memories of the past that matter, but your perception of the American dream. That view becomes a reality in spite of circumstance, location or events. It's finding the ideal place where you can settle down and feel happy. Oak Ridge offered the good life, modeled by parents and grandparents. After graduation, many of my classmates stayed in Oak Ridge because they felt comfortable with familiar patterns."

"Your assumption seems simplistic, but there's your challenge," she suggested. "Sounds like something out of a pop-psychology book, but check out your insight when you go back."

"Yeah, and while I'm at it, I'll see if the old hometown values can accept and forgive *the return of their native son* after all this time. Perhaps, I'll also look for a house in our price range with my good friend Frazier Anderson."

Linda didn't seem amused and left the room without a word.

"The best way to find out
if you can trust somebody
is to trust them."
— Ernest Hemingway

Chapter Five:
Surprise, Surprise, Surprise

"The future you see is the future you get."
— Robert G. Allen

The closer the flight got to Chicago, the more my heart filled with anticipation. Feeling like a reluctant warrior, I thought, Damn, why did I agree to do this*? Perhaps it's a part of growing up and bringing closure to something I've avoided.* I fidgeted like a small child. Sleep avoided me and the in-flight magazine became ink spots on blurred articles. I unbuckled my seatbelt and walked the narrow isle, but couldn't relax.

Too late to turn back now, O'Hare Airport is only an hour away. I started reviewing the list of people I remembered from my senior year and the activities that occupied our time. Sports, cars, dates, hanging out in the summer at Oak Street Beach and the annual trek to Riverview Amusement Park came to mind. It was typical high school fare, but nothing spectacular.

At first, the names and faces of people who threatened to get even with me popped into my head. The nasty telephone calls my parents handled and the physical threats I received made me shudder. Those people successfully filled my dreams with fear and scared me for a long time. *But that happened years ago,* I reasoned. *At my age, I think I'll be safe to go back now.* I turned my thoughts to more pleasant memories of high school.

I remember double dating to the junior prom. My date and I were making out in the back seat of Fred's car when a policeman's flashlight blinded us. We got in trouble for that bit of dancing; they called it necking back then. The forest preserves always offered a great, dark place to take a date. God, I remember that girl sure could kiss ... nice memory. I smiled as I moved aside for a woman heading toward the bathroom and returned to my seat.

I thought of the guy who lived down the street from me, joined the army right after high school. *I wonder if he went to Vietnam.* Then, there was the class joker, Joy, who announced she planned to enroll at the University of Texas to earn a "Mrs. Degree." *It's amazing I could recall those details after all this time.*

I wanted to remember things about all the people on my short list, but the flight attendant's voice interrupted, asking passengers to replace their tray tables and prepare for landing. Once on the ground, I located my luggage and climbed into a waiting taxi. I had booked a room at the Oak Ridge Inn, a village landmark from the past. Growing up, my imagination pictured the inn as an inviting place where only rich people stayed. I envied the hotel's opulence, and whenever I walked past its regal edifice, I promised myself I'd stay there one day. Now, fifty years later, I fulfilled that promise. I hoped the rest of the trip would be this easy.

The receptionist extended a warm greeting and informed me that several former "Oak Ridgers" who had booked rooms in the hotel were hosting a reception in the conference room for early arrivals between 6 and 7 p.m. She handed me a packet of homecoming information, and previous feelings of anxiety disappeared. I headed for my room and smiled at the notion of being in my hometown again. *Yes,* I thought, *this will be an enjoyable weekend.*

I unpacked and sat on the bed to read the contents of the welcome packet. Nothing scheduled today. On Friday, the alumni committee planned to host a cocktail hour and dinner at a local hotel, an intimate place designed to permit old friends and acquaintances to renew friendships.

On Saturday, the continuing celebration coincided with the high school football game. The reunion committee reserved an entire section near the fifty-yard line of the stadium. At half-time, the former homecoming king and queen from our class would be escorted to the middle of the field and honored by the current king and queen. *A bit hokey*, I thought, but it would be the highlight of the afternoon. A dinner and dance at the Oak Ridge Country Club filled the evening hours. Frank, identified as the program's master of ceremonies, would most likely make jokes in his over-the-top fashion and lead us through the program.

Sunday, former classmates from each elementary school arranged breakfast gatherings and photo ops. The schedule, well-planned and appropriately balanced, offered many free hours for friends to enjoy one-on-one conversations.

I called Linda to tell her that I arrived safely, and not to worry about my stress level. She laughed at my discomfort and urged me to enjoy myself. I hung up and headed for the hotel lounge. I walked into the dimly lit room and stood by the bar to let my eyes adjust. I sat down, ordered a Rusty Nail and focused my attention on an attractive brunette sitting at the far end of the bar. I watched the bartender locate the bottles of scotch and Drambuie and heard the woman shout, "Mark …, Mark, is that really you?"

Surprised, I turned to the sound of my name and looked into the sparkling eyes of my junior prom date. "Oh, my god, Celeste! How nice to see you again."

She moved over and gave me a warm hug. Surprisingly, her appearance had not changed much. Celeste had matured and aged some, but all of her familiar mannerisms came flooding back into my memory. She had the habit of tilting her head to the side and smiling with twinkling eyes. She'd begin each sentence with a quick wink. Cute at first, it got old in a hurry. Now it made her look like a frog with something in her eye. In spite of that irritating tic, her lingering touch on my left arm brought back fond memories of our date. I looked at her in amazement. Both of us soaked in the nostalgic moment before we found the words to communicate.

"You look really great, Mark. Time has been kind to you."

"Yeah, a lot of people confuse me with Mel Gibson."

She giggled. "Really? I think you look more like Mel Brooks."

"I see you still have a quick tongue," I said. "Well, even without my glasses, you look terrific, Celeste."

"I give credit to my hairdresser. There are a lot of gray strands hidden beneath this expensive rinse," she quipped with another delightful smile, followed by a wink.

"Give me the CliffsNotes version of your life and tell me what's happened over the past fifty years," I begged. "I know you can't cover it all over a cocktail, but you can hit the highlights. Besides, I'll see you again this weekend."

"For fifty years? Um, the short version is simple: nothing much."

My question easily got her started. I remembered she loved to talk — all the time.

"I settled down in Oak Ridge — married Pete, a guy who moved here from Indiana, opened a floral business, had three kids, bought a house in the suburbs and enjoyed my life. How about you?"

"Wow! That's short and to the point. But, before I share anything about myself, I need to hear more details."

"About what?"

"To start with, you've got to explain why you stayed here in Oak Ridge. I remember you had so many dreams and made a list of places you had to see. Ever make those trips?"

Without a hint of sadness in her voice, she jumped in, "I guess traditions and family ties became more important than any of those old dreams."

I leaned forward, letting my body language encourage her.

"As you know, both my parents were born in Italy. Our family stuck together and relied on each other. It became an expectation."

"Which is?"

"Sticking together. It can be summed up in two words: *family loyalty*. The achievement of our family's American dream turned into a collective affair. My grandmother moved in with Mom and Dad after Grandpa died. They played a major role in raising the kids, and we ended up taking care of them in their old age. My brothers took over the family business and expanded it. When Papa died, the boys turned the restaurant into one of Oak Ridge's most popular destinations. They did really well."

"Why did you let your family loyalty hold you back?"

"Oh, it didn't hold me back." She shot me an incredulous look. "I chose to stay close to them. They needed me. I loved my family and wanted to make them happy. In typical European tradition, the daughter got married and gave them grandchildren. When Pete showed up, my life moved in the expected pattern. I accepted it as my destiny."

"Are you happy with your decision?"

"Oh, yes. I never sacrificed. My family supports me, nurtures my children, and we love spending time together. I wouldn't trade that for anything. I like the community, the schools and the neighborhood. It's a good place to raise a family."

"You don't miss any of those dreams you once had?"

"No. They were," she hesitated to find the right word, "the fantasies of a young girl who didn't realize how good life could be at home with family."

I looked at her quietly, assessing if her decision had brought her happiness or not. However, I chose not to pursue the conversation along those lines. She noticed my silence and abruptly asked, "Aren't you frightened to come back here?"

"Why, should I be?"

"There are still a lot of people who hate you. They don't talk about it anymore, but I know they hold onto those memories."

"That's part of the reason I came back. It's time to take care of that old business while I'm still alive."

"Well, just be cautious, Mark. Don't be surprised if people won't want to talk with you."

"I'll be careful, but I don't think it's that much of a problem, anymore. Thanks for the heads-up, though."

"Now, it's your turn. Tell me what you did after you ran away," she said.

I spent fifteen minutes providing Celeste with the travelogue version of my life's highlights. The words tumbled from my lips like a bubbling brook. I silently thanked Linda for preparing me for this moment. However, soon, Celeste's fidgeting let me know she heard enough. Something told me we had nothing else in common.

In the middle of my Alaskan oil rig story, Celeste suddenly looked at her watch and interrupting said, "Oh, my god, I'm late to pick up my daughter from her dance lesson. Sorry, Mark, I have to scoot."

She grabbed her coat and ran for the door, stopped and turned to face me. "Mark, honestly, I'm surprised to see you're here. Take care. I don't want to see you get hurt."

"Thanks for the warning. I'll pick up the tab."

She waved her hand at me without looking and disappeared.

After our brief encounter, I felt a twinge of sadness and anxiety. I mourned for a nostalgic past I never knew, but felt a twinge of apprehension that people still wanted to threaten me.

I ordered another Rusty Nail and made a note of my encounter with Celeste in a notebook I carried. I'll share this insight with Linda when I go home. I paused and wrote,

> *Celeste never mentioned our date or being arrested on prom night. So much for my memory of being a great kisser.*
>
> *More importantly ... could I be in danger after all this time?*

> "I like to listen. I have learned a great deal from listening carefully. Most people never listen."
> — Ernest Hemingway

Chapter Six:
Building a Nest Egg

"What matters is where you want to go.
Focus in the right direction."
— Donald Trump

The bartender placed a bowl of pretzels in front of me and mixed another drink. Half an hour passed, and the lounge filled with more customers. Looking around for former classmates, I spotted a group of men sitting at a corner table. One of the men looked vaguely familiar, but I wasn't sure. They rose to leave and walked past the bar. One stopped to pay the tab and glanced in my direction. Although the man had put on about fifty pounds and lost most of his hair, I recognized the irritating nasal quality in his voice.

"Tom Milliken, is that you?" I asked.

Puzzled, he looked at me, searching his memory to connect a name with my face.

I assisted him through his awkward moment by saying, "Mark Pierce, we went to high school together."

"Oh, yes, of course, ... Mark. I thought you were some place in Siberia looking for oil."

"True, that happened about thirty years ago."

"Once you left Oak Ridge, we heard only rumors. You became the phantom that a lot of us talked about after high school, and then we forgot you."

Tom always had a direct, blunt way with words, I thought. "I hope that's all water under the bridge ... as they say in polite circles."

"Some people in town still refer to it as 'the flood that took out the bridge,' " he snickered. "It takes a lot of guts for you to come back after your disastrous escapade. I hope you brought your hip waders because the water is still deep in some places. But, you probably don't want to talk about that, either."

"Right. I'd appreciate discussing other things."

"Sure. What are you doing back in Oak Ridge?" He quickly answered his own question. "Don't tell me you were invited to the class reunion?" He smiled.

"Right again. I guess someone made a mistake and sent me an invitation."

He ignored my response and continued, "It should be a good party in spite of your past."

Now it was my turn to disregard his reference and retreat to safer ground.

"Tell me, Tom, what's been happening in your life since high school?"

"Me?"

I watched him puff up with obvious pride that looked almost regal.

"Well, pal," he began.

A colloquial phrase he probably uses with everyone, I thought. *We were never close to being "pals," and he never tried to understand what happened to me in high school. But, today he wants to gloat about his success.* I decided to listen and tilted my head as if I cared.

"I can tell you I've made more money than you could ever imagine — accumulated enough wealth to make life enjoyable, no, let me rephrase that," he continued, "absolutely obscene amounts of money. I can afford everything my family could ever want." Speaking in an arrogant tone and poking me in the chest with his forefinger for emphasis, Tom added, "Enough for today and my kid's foreseeable future." He paused and smirked, "It's been a wonderful trip, and I'm proud of it." Tom searched my eyes for approval.

I looked at the man and expressed my amazement in a single word, "Wow!"

Tom's smug expression let me know he was dying to share his success formula. So, I acquiesced, "How and when did all this happen?"

"I'm glad you asked because it's a fascinating story." Tom sat down on the stool next to me, and we ordered another drink. When the bartender disappeared, he leaned closer to make sure only the two of us heard his highly classified secret. His tale evoked vague memories of what I knew of this man when we were children.

Tommy, as we used to call him back then, moved to Oak Ridge when he entered junior high school. Actually, his prior experiences primed him for life in the Oak Ridge culture, and the city offered him a way to experiment. His parents frequently moved because Tommy's father served in the armed forces and later became an engineer with the Apollo space program. This lifestyle forced Tommy to make new friends quickly, and he had to adjust to changing schools and houses every couple of years. These rapid changes taught him self-confidence and effective people skills.

Shortly after Tommy's arrival in Oak Ridge, he developed a unique talent that foreshadowed his eventual career choice. Tommy loved to collect and count things. At a young age, he practiced all the necessary skills of a trained accountant. He accumulated vast numbers of Good Humor ice cream sticks and saved those with the embossed star. The Good Humor Company offered a free ice cream treat to anyone who returned a novelty stick with the company's logo on it. Tommy sold these sticks to his friends for twenty-five cents.

He'd make a profit, and his friends could get a discount on their next ice cream purchase. Tommy became the neighborhood entrepreneur.

Tommy also collected baseball cards and other treasures and saved them in boxes he stored in his basement. He demonstrated a gift for predicting how the value of some items would increase over time. That hunch paid off and the box of original baseball cards he hoarded eventually sold for ten thousand dollars.

Besides collecting things, Tommy developed a fondness for piggybanks and worked hard to fill his with loose change he found around the house and in the streets, or money he earned by returning bottles and selling junk. In Tommy's pre-adolescent development, collecting things easily translated into investments. Tommy's siblings became his primary investment clients. His older brothers and sisters always needed cash. Whenever they ran out of money, Tommy became their friendly banker offering interest-bearing loans. Frequently, Tommy lent his sister five dollars and expected six in return. His brothers borrowed twenty dollars a week, and Tommy insisted he get repaid twenty-five dollars. If his siblings balked at any deal, he'd threaten to cut off his financial services. His school classmates astutely declined his offers to provide them with a friendly loan. Tommy's practiced usury surprised everyone who unwittingly stepped into his monetary web.

Tommy now explained his rise to financial greatness began when he entered college downstate and earned a business degree. His grades, social network and savvy business reputation landed a job at First National Bank of Oak Ridge. Within a year, he mastered the refined skills of business accounting and corporate leadership. Now addressed as "Mr. Thomas," he established a reputation as an individual with a quick mind, an excellent command of monetary matters and a creative problem solver. In the years that followed, Tom moved through various financial positions and developed a passion and expertise of being a loan officer, mortgage consultant, financial advisor and investment broker.

As the decades unfolded, Mr. Thomas created an extensive professional network, working alongside individuals he had personally helped to establish their own businesses. Many courted Tom as a potential partner, but he remained aloof from such connections. Earning the reputation as Oak Ridge's "golden wizard of finance," he emerged as the sole owner and CEO of a local investment firm.

By the time Tom finished his story, I whistled and added, "Oak Ridge became a very, very lucrative place for you, didn't it?"

"Right you are, Mark. I've made millions, and the city has been a great place to raise my family. I've got it all: sports cars, a cabin in Wisconsin, trips abroad, country club membership and private schools for the kids. I couldn't ask for more."

"Ever think of leaving Oak Ridge and using your talents in a place like Chicago or New York?" I asked.

"Are you kidding me? I've got everything I need here in Oak Ridge. Why would I move to a big city or away from this life? I'd have to work twice as hard for the luxuries I positioned myself to earn here. No, my friend, when you've got it made, you've got it made. Why change things when you're happy?"

"I agree. Life has been terrific for you, Tom."

"Yup, but let's not talk too loud about it. I don't want to jinx the future. I plan to ride out the wave of prosperity and turn the surfboard over to my kids. Then I can retire early and go sit on the beach."

He grinned at me, and I said, "I didn't think they had a Good Humor truck in Hawaii."

Tom didn't smile. He stood up and said, "I know this will seem rude, but I've got to meet my wife and kids downtown for dinner. It's the youngest one's birthday, and I can't be late."

I nodded, letting him know I understood.

"You plan to be at the dinner tomorrow night?" he asked.

"Yes," I smiled. "I'll share my incredible life story with you then."

"Only if you're there long enough to talk. I'll be watching for the fireworks," he said.

"I'll probably rattle a few cages when I make an appearance."

"You most certainly will," he responded, putting on his coat and walking past me.

"I'll see you tomorrow," I shouted after him. "I may need at least one friend at the party." Then I thought, *you've got to be kidding, Mark. Why would that pompous son of a bitch be in your corner tomorrow night?*

Tom used his adult life to amass a great deal of wealth in the comfort of his home town. For Tom, Oak Ridge represented a lucrative place to ply his skills and make millions. I returned to my drink and pictured him in a green leprechaun suit, sitting in his basement counting the coins in his pot of gold. I smiled and then realized, like Celeste, the money man had stiffed me for the drinks.

> "That is what we are supposed to do when we are at our best — make it all up — but make it up so truly that later it will happen that way."
> — Ernest Hemingway

Chapter Seven:
Soaring Without a Net

> "It's not so much that we're afraid of change or so in love with the old ways, but it's that place in-between that we fear .... It's like being between trapezes.
> It's Linus when his blanket is in the dryer.
> There's nothing to hold on to."
> — Marilyn Ferguson

I pulled out a roll of bills and asked the bartender to settle the tab. I received the change and turned to leave. On the way, I practically bumped into Judy Brooks, who was just walking into the bar. She looked at the surprise on my face, grabbed both of my arms and vigorously shook me.

"I can't believe it — it's you," she said and then added, "You certainly have a lot of damn nerve returning for this class reunion, don't you?"

Slack-jawed, I looked at her. "I guess if you think so." I then stepped backward to escape from her clutch. "Let me look at you. Age has been kind to you — a little heavier around the middle and graying like the rest of us."

She invaded my space again and pushed back my hair. "Those scars on your forehead healed nicely. Lucky for you, mister."

Her physical confrontation and caustic words stung more than I could have imagined. Judy always had a sarcastic way of delivering backhanded compliments and a biting tongue to enhance every occasion.

"It looks as if you haven't changed much, either, Judy. Still angry as ever. Probably had lots of time to practice."

"Yeah, life still sucks, and it will stay that way as long as people like you don't take responsibility for your actions."

Ignoring her attempt to engage me in a fifty-year-old argument, I sidestepped her biting comment and smiled. "I assume you're here for the class reunion, too."

"Right, but I'm not a visitor like some people who blow in with the wind. I can honestly call Oak Ridge my home."

I tried to raise the level of our conversation and transition into a civil discussion between adults who once knew each other. Linda and I rehearsed this kind of approach in case I needed a diversion. I smiled and feigned interest. "I thought you went to New York to become an actress."

"I did ... and the whole trip was a waste of my time. You have no idea how hostile New York can be." Still playing the role of a high-drama martyr, her acid tongue ignored my past and focused on the misery in her life. "They lie," she continued, "pump a young girl's head full of fairytale dreams and then walk away. I felt like I got chewed up and spit out by those theatrical vultures that prey on blossoming talent."

I remembered Judy starred in every stage production and theater event produced in junior high and high school. Her inflated ego, nurtured by friends, turned her into a stuck-up, self-centered, haughty bitch all through school. The image of her self-proclaimed magnificence being ignored and tuned out by Broadway critics made the corners of my mouth turn up, but I suppressed the smile. *At least she's content to talk about herself and not rip on me,* I thought.

Judy's mother pushed her into acting classes at a young age, and then forced her into singing and dancing lessons in junior high. She worked hard at refining her limited talent. Living the vicarious dreams of her parents, she became good, but never outstanding. With the strength of her irritating personality and nasty attitude, I assumed she would become one of the graduates who successfully transitioned into the bigger world outside of Oak Ridge.

For a moment, I felt a smidge of compassion and asked, "What happened in New York to bring you back here?"

"Oh, god, what didn't happen? The agent who *discovered me* scheduled several auditions, but I never landed a good part. I did a lot of off-Broadway theater, but the big break never came. In short, nobody of importance recognized my talent as an actress, and I finally returned to my sanity."

Found by a theatrical agent when she performed the lead role of *Kiss Me Kate*, a modern high school version of Shakespeare's play, she impressed him with her magnificent voice and great stage presence. As an actress, she played every role with a believable quality. However, after the play, the off-stage Judy turned into the egotistical girl I remember as a classmate. The role of Katharina in *Kiss Me Kate* never challenged her acting skills — too much like her personality in real life — too realistic. It didn't qualify as *acting*.

"So, you got discouraged with the job prospects and came home?"

"No, the culture of New York drove me home," her voice quivered

I looked at her with a puzzled expression, and she jumped at the chance to explain.

"Here's how life worked in New York in the 1960s. You moved into an apartment and installed six or seven locks on doors and windows, and if you didn't get robbed in the first two weeks, you had found a safe neighborhood. Not exactly a description that inspires confidence when compared to a small city like Oak Ridge."

"Right," I interjected, "I remember the days when some people here never locked their doors at night and left the keys in their cars. You're telling me that not being robbed in New York defined the meaning of safety?"

"Yeah, and I always felt uncomfortable on the street. I never developed that personal space, the isolated shell thing to keep me distant and aloof from other people. Finally, I moved to the suburbs and tried commuting."

"How did that work?"

"Strip malls lined both sides of the streets. You couldn't tell where one suburb ended and another began unless you listened to people's accents to see which ethnic neighborhood you wandered into. Cultural identity fears and desires isolated people from each other. The Big Apple only showed me a *worm hole*, and I had to crawl out through it. Not a pretty picture."

"It's quite a leap from Oak Ridge, where you know everyone, to a large multicultural city filled with strangers," I added.

"I really missed the life we enjoyed during our high school years. The sense of community invited people into the streets to chat with their neighbors, especially when the Good Humor truck came around. In New York, it became too dangerous for the Good Humor man to drive his truck in certain parts of the city." She hesitated and added, "Kids robbed the ice cream man. How can life be okay if a street vendor in charge of an American institution gets rolled for his change and ice cream?" she concluded.

Judy paused to add a sense of drama to her impromptu stage performance. For a second, I believed she could have even shed a tear. However, her delay offered a dramatic moment to deliver her final line and take a curtain call. "I moved back here after spending eight years in hell. Such a waste of my life."

"What are you doing now?"

"I am the director of the Community Arts Center, run the gallery and local theatrical productions six times a year. I have an incredible job, and they pay me to do what I love best — to act.

"I assume you like living back in Oak Ridge now?"

"Are you kidding me?" she offered. "I live in a neighborhood with green lawns, close to shopping, near work and less than an hour from the amenities of Chicago. Best of all, I know all of my neighbors and feel connected — like it felt in high school. Twice a year, we even have block parties."

"It sounds like you've discovered an ideal life here," I responded.

Just then, a man approached Judy and gave her a quick hug. She jumped, but relaxed when she recognized her husband's touch. Judy briefly introduced me to Alex and said they planned to meet another couple for dinner. I exchanged awkward pleasantries with him.

I thought the conversation had successfully diverted her wrath, but before Judy walked away, she turned back to me and slipped in a final, scratchy comment. "I look forward to watching you squirm at the reception tomorrow night. It will be fun to see you get what you deserve."

I offered a weak smile and concluded the less I say now, or see her again this weekend the better it will be for my peace of mind. I knew my presence in Oak Ridge would be broadcast throughout the "proverbial grapevine" before the end of the evening and others would have plenty to chew on before the party began. Watching the couple walk into the hotel's dining room, I saw Judy holding a cell phone to her ear. *She's probably announcing her discovery of my arrival to the first grape on the vine now,* I thought.

I opened my notebook and summarized the unexpected conversations I had with former classmates.

> *Perception of happiness is an individual thing, but places like Oak Ridge don't offer enough "solace"*

to change people's personalities. They can be spiteful no matter where they live.

Suddenly, I felt lonely and tired. An uneasy feeling of dread seeped into my mind. *Perhaps I made a mistake about deciding to come back,* I thought. *It may have been a fantasy to think I could turn things around. This may not work ... probably best to skip the Oak Ridger's reception tonight.*

"If you have a success you have it for the wrong reasons. If you become popular it is always because of the worst aspects of your work."
— Ernest Hemingway

Chapter Eight:
Touch of the Familiar

"There is nothing like staying at home for real comfort."
— Jane Austen

Coming to Oak Ridge had already bombarded my mind and body with information overload — too much for a guy isolated from his hometown for the past fifty years. Unexpectedly tired, I returned to my room and took a long shower. After drying off, I still felt fatigued from the long day and the first challenging conversations with former classmates. My diplomatic, soft approach had drained much of my energy. Wrapped in the soft cotton robe provided by the hotel, I sprawled on the bed and fell asleep.

When I awoke, it was past seven and darkness added to the surreal images of shadows from streetlights shining into my room. I stretched, studied the ceiling fan rotating in the dim light and assessed the value of the trip so far. With no effort on my part, I had connected with a couple of former classmates in the hotel bar. I learned about their life choices and discovered one of them was still angry with me. The second looked forward to someone punching me out, and Celeste — my former prom date — seemed to be too distracted by her own world. *Well,* I thought, *that wasn't a total negative vibe. At least they all talked with me. I may be able to survive this event without additional scars.*

I climbed out of bed, and pangs of hunger grabbed my attention. I decided Franklin's Pizza Villa and Ice Cream Shoppe on Lake Street begged for my presence. A touch of melancholy and the recollection of fond after-school memories made my mouth water for a taste of their pizza and a sweet, confectionary after-dinner treat. In those days, every time someone ordered a large sundae, it was delivered to the table with lit red, white and blue sparklers. The thick pizza, covered with a sweet tomato sauce and lots of mozzarella cheese, turned an ordinary Italian dish into a culinary feast.

Enthusiastically, I dressed in a pair of khaki slacks, a black T-shirt and a corduroy coat — casual, but appropriate for a Thursday evening. To my delight, the restaurant looked about the same as it did fifty years ago. I instantly felt comfortable reliving activities that filled many of my high school evenings. Franklin's succulent food temporarily soothed my remaining anxiety about the reunion. Given my age and smaller appetite, I could only manage a single-scoop cone after dinner and sat outside on their bench to enjoy every lick.

When I finished, the warm Midwestern evening invited me to meander through the village I once called home. The peaceful night reminded me of another occasion that caused Linda and me to have our first fight. Ironically, our disagreement occurred in the quiet of another town much like Oak Ridge.

We had just started dating and learning about each other. On a road trip through the southwest, we stopped in a small Arizona city named Safford, a sleepy town where residents took pride in boasting about their two seasons: *summer*, from May through October when the daily temperatures tops three digits, and *non-summer*, when it wasn't quite as hot. Some people even claimed it snowed there in January, but I'm convinced that's an urban myth. People in Safford earned a living by working in the nearby copper mines or by farming and ranching.

After checking into a motel, Linda and I headed for dinner at a local restaurant. The plastic nametag on our waitress stated: *Hi. My name is Faye, welcome*!

Jumping at the chance to make a friendly connection I said, "Out of curiosity, Faye, how long have you lived in Safford."

"All my life, why do you ask?"

"I don't understand why anyone would want to stay out here in such isolation?"

Linda elbowed my side, but Faye answered without hesitation.

"My parents lived here all of their lives and so did my grandparents. I met my husband in high school, and he got a great job in the copper mines over in Globe. It's only a twenty-mile drive from our house. I've been a waitress in this restaurant for fifteen years and love people because I know most of them."

"That sounds like a very pleasant life to me," Linda said.

"No offense, Faye, but it sounds boring as hell," I added. "It's as exciting as watching paint dry or grass grow. That is, if any grass could survive in this heat. How do people have fun in this town?"

Without realizing what I was saying, my innocent questions and caustic remarks strayed into an uncomfortable value conflict between Linda and me.

"Don't cause trouble, Mark," Linda chided.

"I'm not offended, ma'am," Faye responded. "We lead a simple life and don't need a lot of entertainment. Every Friday night, most of the locals head for the bowling alley, roll a few lanes, drink beer and socialize. It's either that or they play bingo at the Legion Hall. If you throw in a dinner at a restaurant or go to a movie, you call it a weekend."

"That kind of life would be too quiet for me. I need to be around people, bars, action," I countered.

"I'd give up the rat race of San Francisco any day to have some time in a pastoral setting like this. No worries, laid-back, relaxed and, best of all, you know everyone in town," Linda said.

"If that's the case," I snipped, "then our relationship will be short-lived. You'll never catch me living in the boondocks."

"That statement was uncalled for, Mark." Linda's tone grew icy. "If you mean it, we've got a problem."

"Absolutely, and I can't understand why you'd choose to give up San Fran for a place like this."

"I'd trade city life … and my relationship with you for that matter … to plant a garden, raise a few animals, hike the hills, fish and camp. This kind of setting offers enough peace to soothe the soul."

"But, you can't live on fresh air alone, Linda." Then, turning to Faye, I asked, "Does Safford provide everything you need?"

"No, you can't expect that in such a small town," she said thoughtfully. "Once a month, my husband and I jump in the pickup and head toward Phoenix. We stop at Super Wal-Mart in Apache Junction about fifty miles away, load up with supplies for the month, buy some clothes or maybe go to dinner. That's a nice treat."

"That's it?" I said. "Linda, that kind of life would drive me crazy. You'd have to move here alone."

"Oh, stop it, Mark. I'm sure you'd adjust and love it." She poked at my arm. "Faye, what's the best thing locals do around here?"

"Um," she thought. "Well, besides fishing and hunting, there's always Annie's Hot Springs?"

Linda perked up. "What's Annie's Hot Springs? It sounds interesting."

"Listen, Linda, don't get all cozy with the idea of an idyllic lifestyle in a small town. I know I couldn't do it."

"Come on, Mark. Open your mind to the possibilities."

"I think you'd like Annie's," Faye added. "She and her husband started a commune on a patch of land near town and discovered hot springs on it. They turned it into a nice little business we all appreciate."

"Oh, great, let's go back in time and find a hippie commune," I said.

On Saturday morning, Linda and I followed Faye's obscure directions and traveled on back roads to Annie's place. True to my expectations, Annie's Hot Springs reminded me of the late 1960s. A small sign announced, *Hot Springs Soaks, $5.00 per person/per hour.* Four small sheds, each painted in wild colors of pink, blue, purple and chartreuse, sat on top of hot springs that bubbled up from the ground beneath each one.

I paid our host the ten-dollar fee and asked, "How often do people use the hot springs?"

"Most of the locals come out on the weekends," Annie said. "The springs were once a well-kept secret from outsiders, but now we get tourists like you dropping in all the time. It's a good place to bring a date, get naked and play. People can socialize and enjoy an hour or two of relaxation. A few couples have even used our springs for their wedding reception."

Linda and I occupied the blue shed and eavesdropped on the conversations and sounds of laughter coming from the other huts.

The warm waters took the edge off my irritation with this adventure, and I relaxed enough to focus on talking to Linda about our obvious differences.

"Do you seriously think you could enjoy this kind of lifestyle?" I asked.

"Yes, I often feel too confined in a large city like San Francisco. I grew up on a ranch and miss the space and freedom."

"But you know I am serious. I could never live in a place like this," I said.

"I know," she laughed. "You'd go nuts with all the silence."

"Right, I couldn't do it — even for you — and I love you."

"I know, and I promise not to push this sort of lifestyle on you."

"Thanks. I know some people feel comfortable living out predictable patterns, and others, like me, are curious about what's waiting around the next corner."

I remembered that our talk about the merits of living in a sedate town like Safford could have been a deal breaker for us, but the trip turned into a defining moment. We agreed to stay together in San Francisco, but promised to give each other space and time to pursue our separate needs. We agreed that Linda would go camping alone in the wilderness whenever the desire kicked in; and I'd take side trips to explore the new places I'd read about in the paper or online. She'd often accompany me, but I made it clear I was a city boy and not the Daniel Boone type.

The compromise worked for us and helped clarify our own sense of comfort with our diverse needs. I wonder what life would have been like if I had stayed in Oak Ridge. The town retains the quiet of a rural setting, but is close enough to Chicago to enjoy all the urban amenities. *I wonder if I should look up Frazier Anderson and let him show me some houses*, I smiled at the thought. *Nope, not this time.*

But Oak Ridge, I grinned, *would definitely challenge the peace and contentment of the Safford residents — slightly more wild than getting naked and going for a soak at Annie's.*

> "But life isn't hard to manage when you've nothing to lose."
> — Ernest Hemingway

Chapter Nine:
Devine Insight

"Our lives improve only when we take chances and the first and most difficult risk we can take is to be honest with ourselves."
— Walter Anderson

On the walk through the park back to my hotel, I started to feel comfortable with my former home again. Oak Ridge, like Safford, had always been an oasis — a safe island — for people who wanted — no, needed — to be surrounded by predictable patterns. *It must be that way in a lot of places,* I thought.

I sat on a quaint, wooden park bench, a throwback from a bygone era, and enjoyed the moon flickering on the pond in front of me. Memories of bringing girls here for romantic dates filled my mind, and I only looked up as an older gentlemen approached. His physical features and unique gait revealed his identity.

"Excuse me, sir, are you Father McCray?"

"Yes, I am. And who might you be?"

"After all these years, you may not recognize me. I'm Mark Pierce."

"Oh, my goodness, I'm pleased to see you again, especially after what happened to you in high school."

"Yes, it's me. To put it in religious terms, this weekend I'm playing the return of the prodigal son."

He chuckled. "Well, may God bless you, Mark. I always felt so bad about your choice to leave. Kids can be very cruel at that age."

"I've discovered people can still be cruel at any age."

He smiled and agreed.

"Thank you, Father," I continued. "I have worked through a lot of things in life and now want to clear up the sins of the past. That's one of the reasons I came back to our fiftieth reunion."

"Good for you, my son. A class reunion is a good place to seek forgiveness. There is a reason God brought you here. As I always say, God works in mysterious ways."

"Still quoting from the old hymnal, Father? Does that mean you're still preaching at St. Mary's?"

"Oh, no, my son, I retired several years ago. I'm almost ninety," he smiled. "The fire I once had in my soul is now only glowing embers."

"You look very good, Father." Thinking my former priest would have a unique insight about the people who lived here, I delved deeper than our surface pleasantries. "You've lived and worked in Oak Ridge for quite a long time. Perhaps you can help me understand what I missed."

"Sure. What do you want to know?"

"I believe a lot of my former classmates chose to live in Oak Ridge after they graduated. Do you know why they chose to stay?"

"Oh, that's easy. When I had a chance to talk about life with parishioners, many of them expressed a fear of change. To comfort my flock, I used to preach about those fears in my sermons, but I don't think it made a difference. I know that fear grips people — freezes their minds and holds them in place."

"What kind of fear will do that?"

"It has been my experience that certain fears about the unknown limit people's willingness to risk."

"Can you give me an example, Father?" I asked.

"I can honestly say their anxieties can be reduced to three paralyzing fears: fear of failure, fear of financial limitations and fear of perception."

"Go on, Father."

"Of course, if you have time for an old man?"

"For you, Father, I have as much time as you need."

"Mark, I have learned that the fear of failure is humanity's biggest limitation." He paused and stared into my face.

I wonder if this is a personal message to me, I thought.

"People fear failure because they don't want friends or family to make judgments about their folly. From early childhood, we watched the emotional embarrassment that came when some poor soul got picked last to play on an intramural team in gym class. People snickered at the *loser* in the group. Children can be mean-spirited, and unfortunately, the fear of being inadequate carries over into adulthood. Adults don't want to be seen as the last one chosen to play on the team of life."

"You're telling me that fear of being ridiculed — making bad choices — limit options?"

"Absolutely. For many, taking a risk and doing something outside accepted norms holds them up for ridicule, shame or jocularity. Nobody wants to be judged because they make a stupid decision, fail and have a negative impact on their future."

"They judge you even if your mistake is an accident."

"People pay a huge price for failure and cause them to fear the social and emotional fallout. Nobody enjoys being the grist of social conversations. Judgment prevents growth."

He let the words sink in for me and abruptly added, "So, tell me, Mark, you took a risk with your life, how did you finally address your fears?"

"You thought I left Oak Ridge out of fear, Father?"

"My son, nobody leaves with unresolved issues like yours without being afraid."

Our conversation lapsed into silence. I looked at Father McCray, who had closed his eyes as if in prayer. I had no idea how to respond. *How did he know so much?* I thought. I took a deep breath and exhaled loudly through my pursed lips. "I never knew you followed our lives so closely."

"Mark, as your parish priest, the happiness of my flock had always been important to me."

"How did you know about my personal struggle?"

"You left us so suddenly and everyone talked about it. I spent many hours praying for your soul. I could imagine you spending years wandering about, alone with all of your accumulated guilt. Your presence today has answered my prayers."

"Thank you, Father. I know I have a lot of work to do this weekend, but don't know where to begin."

"Trust in your heart, Mark. God, in all his abundance will provide the answer."

Uncomfortable with the direction the conversation was heading, I returned to his thoughts on people's motives for staying in Oak Ridge. I gently reminded him to finish by saying, "Speaking of abundance, Father, you said people don't take risks because of the fear of financial failure."

"I'm sorry. I became distracted. Forgive the wanderings of an old priest."

"I'm impressed by your insights. Please continue."

"Yes, most people see the world as if it had limited resources, and they fear financial loss or poverty."

"You mean most people see their part of the world as the half-empty glass?"

"Exactly. From a religious perspective, abundance is not something we acquire in life, but something we tune into. But too many of my parishioners chose to hide their talents for a rainy day."

"People put off living — delay experiencing life because they fear the lack of abundance," I added.

"Yes, and many people fear they do not have enough resources to handle an emergency — an emergency that may never come."

I thought about his words and asked for a clarification of the final fear that keeps people in one place. "Father, help me understand what you mean by fear of perception."

"People often fear the unknown or accept perceptions of what they think they know about a place or thing. Such fear paralyzes action."

"I'm not sure I understand, Father," I said.

"Most people pretend to know what's out in the world. This pretense is based on limited information that makes them feel like 'experts' about what other places can offer — lifestyle, weather, jobs or culture."

"You mean like using Wikipedia as the absolute truth because it's on the Internet?"

"Yes," he smiled. "Mention moving to Colorado and people say, 'Too much snow for me.' In reality, only the mountains accumulate great depths of snow. When the Chinook winds blow along the Front Range, most of the snow disappears within days, if not hours. The altitude is so high even the most ferocious blizzard leaves few traces after a couple days of sunshine. So, the perception that Colorado is totally covered with snow is an error, but it dominates people's thinking and drives their choices."

"I guess it's like that with a lot of things," I said. "Actually, most people know less about what's actually over the next hill than they think they do."

We both smiled, and Father McCray continued.

"So, my son, your choice to leave us opened a whole new world for you, didn't it? Many of my parishioners will travel to faraway places, but may never see the positive aspects or creativity to be found in different cultures. Often myth and legend gets in the way."

Father McCray took a deep breath and stopped talking. In the silence of his wisdom, I observed his body begin to tire. It was time to end the discussion. He stood up and said, "I'm glad we had this time together. I hope my thoughts helped you." We shared a brief hug, and he wished me well with a quick blessing.

I sat on the bench thinking about his perceptions and wisdom. From my extensive experiences moving about the world, I discovered unlimited possibilities and chose to pursue most of them. *What does it take*, I wondered, *for a person to overcome the fears Father McCray identified and break out of their comfort zone?*

Filled with understanding from the highest religious source I knew in Oak Ridge, I retired for the night with the hope that I'd find other classmates who could answer that question.

"Every man's life ends the same way. It is only the details of how he lived and how he died that distinguish one man from another."
— Ernest Hemingway

Chapter Ten: Childhood Allusions

"Old friends make the best antiques."
— U.S. postage stamp

A warm fall sun flooded my room and welcomed me to Friday morning in Oak Ridge. After a shower, I looked into the mirror and decided my appearance needed attention. My laid-back, San Francisco look required more polish for this weekend's celebration.

I gazed again into the bathroom mirror to study my features. My thick, brown hair provided enough cover in front to hide the once-nasty scars across my forehead. It tumbled down the back of my head and rested in small curls on my shoulders. I inspected the abundant gray streaks that now peppered it and dominated my short sideburns. They reminded me of two white beacons framing a weathered, ancient shoreline. "Oh, you will look so distinguished as your hair turns gray, Mark," Linda often said in an encouraging way. *Nonsense!* I thought. My once full mustache was now thinning and mostly white. So, I took the time to shave it off.

"You're getting old, Mark," I spoke to my reflection as I washed off remnants of shaving cream. "Even my famous image is fading. Mel, where have you gone?" *I need to visit a barbershop and have this mane trimmed and evened out to look more professional,* I thought. *I may live in California, but I don't want to be mistaken for an old hippie.*

The face in the mirror revealed laugh wrinkles around my eyes and the image that looked back barely resembled my graduation picture. My face had filled out over time — the result of a life filled with delicious food and splendid wines. However, I still looked about ten years younger than my sixty-seven years indicated. My smile and flashing delphinium eyes occasionally turned the head of an admiring female.

I patted my stomach and made a mental note to start working out again. My sedate lifestyle in the bookstore created the beginnings of a slight paunch and noticeable love handles. "Funny, Linda hasn't said anything about these yet."

Well, Mark, after a light breakfast of fruit and Special K, you need to walk down to the shopping area, find a barbershop and buy a dress shirt for tonight's party.

Satisfied with my new purchases, I emerged from the men's store and headed for the barbershop and almost bowled over a red-haired woman coming around the corner. She immediately recognized me.

"Mark Pierce, look at you … all grown up and mature!"

"Sort of like Mel Gibson?"

"No, not even close, Worm. What brings you back into Oak Ridge?"

"Small world, isn't it, Marie?" I responded. "I'm back for my class reunion and really glad to see a favorite friend from my past."

"You sure look a lot better today than the last time I saw you," she smiled. Then she hit me on the arm, a gesture that reminded me of Linda. "It's been fifty years and no word from you, Worm. I stopped by your house to see you when you were recuperating, but your parents didn't tell me you were leaving. Then, the week after graduation, they told me you left for places unknown." With both hands on her hips, she shouted, "Is that a way to treat your closest childhood friend?"

"I'm sorry, Marie. I had to leave, and didn't say goodbye to anyone."

"You should be sorry, Mr. Hotshot. I was one of the few people who stuck by you when all the shit went down," she pouted.

I smiled at her dramatic response and gave her a warm hug. "It's really good to see you again, Red. Got some time to talk?"

"Don't you try to leave without talking to me. We're practically brother and sister. How about the coffee shop across the street?"

Marie, a year younger than me, had lived three houses down the block. We grew up playing together, but never dated or explored any romantic connection. A fiery redhead, always quick to anger, Marie may have been the most precocious girl I ever met. We road bikes and played cars and other childhood games, but as puberty set in, the games got serious. Naively, I always assumed girls were just lumpy boys — clueless about anything related to gender differences or sex. Marie matured early and changed all that. One Saturday, Marie, Don, Carrie, Jack and I were playing in Marie's basement when she suggested, "Let's play a new game called: I'll show you mine, if you show me yours."

I had no idea how to play or what new territory we were exploring, but it sounded like fun.

"Who wants to go first?" Marie asked.

"Me, me," I yelled, waving my hand in the air like this was some school project.

"Okay, everyone except Mark has to wait on the other side of the room. But we'll all have a turn, just one at a time."

Carrie must have sensed the game's impropriety and ran upstairs and out of the house. Don and Jack walked to the other side of the basement, but strained their necks to peek at the action.

I stood in front of Marie, and she pulled down her pants to reveal a very small patch — a fluff — of bright red hair. I gazed at it in amazement. Then, she announced, "Okay, your turn."

I slipped my jeans and underpants almost to my knees and held a soft penis between my fingers. She reached over and wiggled it. However, at that moment, Marie's father opened the basement door and yelled down the stairs, "Hey, what are you kids doing down there?"

In unison, all of us nervously responded, "Nothing."

Frantically, Marie and I pulled up our pants, and she smiled at me. The naughty thrill of the game transformed us into best friends. Our little escapade created an unspoken bond of secrecy. After the experience in her basement, I affectionately called Marie, "Red," and, in turn, she nicknamed me "Worm."

Now, as I sat across from her drinking coffee, I warmly remembered Marie as my first intimate adventure with a girl. I set my cup down and flashed a large Cheshire cat grin. Marie removed a trace of whip cream from her lips and noticed my smug look.

"What are you smiling about, Mark?"

"Oh, just remembering the past. You and I go back a long way. Tell me, did you ever get married?"

"Yeah, I married Kyle Brock. He was two years younger than you and dropped out of school in his senior year to work in the mill. I finished high school and got a job at the cosmetics counter at Marshall Fields, downtown. Mom and Dad loved Kyle, and they encouraged us to get married. Three years later, we bought a house about six blocks from where they lived. We would have started a family had Kyle not taken ill."

"What happened?" I inquired.

"Kyle started having trouble breathing and then developed a cough that wouldn't go away. Finally, medical tests diagnosed him with an advanced case of tuberculosis."

"Oh, no," I exclaimed in astonishment. "What did you do?"

"We followed doctor's orders and headed to a drier climate — moved to Arizona and got treatment at one of those specialized clinics."

"That must have been a difficult, if not a heart-wrenching decision for you — moving away and all."

"It was the most difficult thing I have ever done in my life. We were so close to our parents. My mom and dad were absolutely distraught and our friends devastated. We had to quit our jobs and start again in a strange place."

"How did you handle it?"

"To tell you the truth, Mark, it was like going through all the stages of death and dying. We felt waves of grief, followed by periods of denial, and then ended up in outright anger. We were on an emotional roller coaster. All of our life plans were put on hold as we tried to deal with Kyle's health issues."

"Wow. It must have been extremely hard."

"You know, our parents thought we'd only be gone for a short while, and they could visit, or we'd come back on frequent trips. But, none of that ever occurred. We abandoned our friends, family and church community. We sold our house at a loss and left in a financial hole."

Marie stopped to sip her coffee. I watched her eyes fill with tears and her neck breakout in red, tension-induced blotches. I sat quietly, letting her regain composure. She dabbed the edge of her napkin at the tears that now overflowed from the corners of her eyes. She desperately fought to hold them back to protect her mascara from running. She took a deep breath and continued.

"Then, things got bad."

"How could it get worse than that?"

"Kyle couldn't get work, and his health continued to decline. We received word that his insurance benefits had maxed out. On top of that, his family was hit with two other tragedies. Right after we moved, his sister was killed in a car accident, and his father suddenly died from a heart attack. Kyle couldn't handle any more. He lost all hope."

Now more tears flowed freely down her cheeks, followed by light brown rivulets of mascara. Marie couldn't keep up with the rivers of salty liquid and sat softly weeping with her head in her hands. I reached across the table and placed a comforting hand on her shoulder.

"I'm so sorry, Red."

She looked up and managed a weak smile though her tears. Marie choked in a couple of breaths, trying to gain control. She swished around the remains of her coffee and studied the dark mixture.

"You don't have to share any more if it's too difficult, Marie."

"No, no, you've got to know the rest." She took one last sip of the now insipid liquid, swallowed hard, inhaled deeply and stared into my face. "Kyle couldn't handle it — went sort of crazy. He resigned himself to death and wanted to go out screaming in a self-indulgent orgy. Kyle emotionally abandoned me."

"I don't understand," I said.

"One day Kyle was the loving, caring man I cherished — the one I married. The next, he had completely changed. Kyle tapped out our savings and spent it all at strip clubs, drinking and gambling. He'd disappear for weekends — fly out to Las Vegas and blow more cash he got from credit card withdrawals."

"Sounds like your husband went on a hedonistic binge."

"He'd get angry and refused to discuss it. The harder Kyle played, the worse his health became. Then one day, he didn't get out of bed and told me he planned to die. I thought his behavior was bizarre, and I refused to pay attention to him."

"Did he ever change?"

"No, that's the real tragedy." Marie stopped and wept into her napkin. I held her hand and waited. She finally regained composure and continued. "On the fourth day of Kyle's self-declared deathwatch, he asked me to hold him. He apologized for his behavior and told me death was near." She stopped talking and took in more deep breaths.

After a few moments, I asked, "Did he?"

"Oh, yes. It was as if he willed death to take him. I held Kyle in my arms throughout the night, and when I woke in the morning, he had passed. Nothing I could say or do changed his mind."

"Oh, my god, that's terrible." I stood up and put my arms around Marie. Her body melted into my embrace and remained riveted to my chest without moving. Customers glanced in our direction or walked carefully around us. They kindly gave us the space to share our poignant moment without interruption.

At last, I whispered into her ear, "I'm sorry I wasn't here for you."

"I know. You broke our childhood pledge to be there for each other. I counted on you for support. You deserted your closest friend, and I was angry at you for a long time. Whenever you needed my support, even after you got hurt, I was always there for you. When I needed my best friend, you were nowhere to be found."

Her words ripped at my heart and flooded it with guilt. This is the kind of hurt I wanted to avoid. I cursed my decision to return. I wanted to run back to the hotel and get on the next flight home. "I feel so bad, Marie and promise to be a better friend in the future."

"Thanks, Mark, I appreciate that. But, back then I felt so alone and had to come back home to find myself again."

The heavy conversation about Marie's tragedy dwarfed any discussion we could have had about my life. The emotional tension hung in the air like a thundercloud, and I decided to play my role as consoling friend and not a travelogue guide through my past.

Marie recovered as we chatted about the weekend and other mundane topics. Eventually, we walked out into the late morning sun. We exchanged e-mail addresses and promised to stay in touch.

Marie was a childhood friend who made a commitment to come back to the sanctuary of Oak Ridge for personal support. I wasn't there for her, but promised it wouldn't happen again. We embraced and said goodbye.

I walked back to my hotel thinking of Marie's dilemma. Her news depressed my spirit. *Would my presence have made a difference for her? That's an impossible question to answer because I was elsewhere.*

I reached the hotel, and the doorman's greeting ended my philosophical thoughts about the meaning of life. Pangs of hunger made me realize lunch called, and I pictured myself pouring a cold one and ordering a sandwich in the bar.

"If two people love each other,
there can be no happy end to it."
— Ernest Hemingway

Chapter Eleven:
Discovering an Inca Secret

"A moment's insight is sometimes worth
a life's experience."
— Oliver Wendell Holmes

By four p.m., I had cleaned up and put on my new duds. I spotted my image in the polished door of the elevator as I rode down to the lobby. *You still look okay for an old high school kid.* I pulled the invitation to the reception out of my coat pocket and read the fine print. I was an hour early — enough time to enjoy a cocktail and chat with the bartender. I ordered a Rusty Nail and began to fret about what might happen during the evening.

I looked at my notebook and reviewed the names of people I had already talked with since my arrival. Those people, even Father McCray, glowed about their connection to Oak Ridge. I'd seen the excitement — the sparkle in their eyes, as they talked about friends, family and the community. I didn't understand such loyalty to a town.

I put my pen down and suddenly felt a strange sense of homesickness for a place I had never lived as an adult. A rush of sadness washed over me as I thought about a life that might have been different if I had chosen to remain a part of this community. In a way, I envied classmates who had found peace and contentment in this little box called Oak Ridge.

I let the feeling pass and fondly remembered that first year of backpacking in Europe. "No, I was different," I said between clenched teeth, "cut from a cloth that inspired wanderlust. I can almost appreciate the event that forced me to flee."

Nobody was near enough to hear my ramblings, but the words stimulated my thinking. I returned to my notebook and drew a box in the center of a blank page and labeled it "The Oak Ridge Comfort Zone." On all four of its sides, I placed the words: friends, family, job, money, church, shopping, patterns, home, schools, and community services. In a way, the box represented a symbol to explain why people chose to stay in or near the confines of Oak Ridge. Supported by Father McCray's fear-of-change theory, I now had a better understanding why people settled in, found tranquility and spent an inordinate amount of effort enhancing their nest.

I looked at my drawing and wondered why would people ever choose to leave such a self-created paradise? I pondered my question for a few minutes. *Perhaps,* I thought challenging my mind, *it has to do with the small hole — a crack that exists in everyone's box — a visible opening on one of its protective walls.* "But," I started talking aloud again, "we often attempt to ignore the hole and hide it by placing ... let's say ... a picture or a curtain over it — trying to pretend it doesn't exist." Now animated, I made a few scratches on one of the walls of the box I had drawn. My mumbling and animation drew the attention of the bartender.

"Can I help you, sir?"

"Perhaps. What's your name?"

"Joseph Duggan, ... and yours?"

"Mark Pierce. I'm here for my fiftieth high school reunion."

"I graduated from Oak Ridge myself, but only ten years ago."

"Well, tell me, Joseph, have you ever had the urge, the desire to leave Oak Ridge ... to get out of here?"

"Yes, but I gave that up a long time ago. I had to take care of my parents who were in ill health. I got this job and met my fiancée ... well, you know how that goes, don't you, Mark?"

"Yeah, I'm beginning to understand more and more with every passing day."

Joseph brought me another Rusty Nail and began to study my drawing. We chatted about my idea, and he expressed interest in my theory. Finally, I looked at Joseph and said, "Remember when you were a small child and had a secret dream to go exploring somewhere?"

He nodded in agreement.

"Where did you want to go?"

Joseph thought for a minute and searched his memory, but experienced difficulty recalling his childhood desire. Finally, he smiled and said, "You know, Mark, when I was in the third grade, I watched a special on television about the Inca city of Machu Picchu. You know, the one hidden in the Andes?"

"Yeah, I recall explorers didn't find the city until the twentieth century."

"I always wanted to go there, but never had the time or the money. As a kid, I researched the Incas and fantasized about making the trek up the Andes to explore the site. Then, I went to high school and became distracted with sports and girls."

"You provided me with the perfect symbol for my drawing, Joseph!" I said excitedly. I drew a mountain on the page to the right of my box and labeled it "Machu Picchu."

Joseph looked at me with questioning eyes.

Interrupting his thinking, I said, "You see, Joseph, I believe everyone once had a Machu Picchu dream, formulated in our childhood, but never realized as an adult. As our lives got cluttered with other things — school, job, relationships — we never pursued the dream. Worse, we may have accepted something less. Yet, if you squint through the crack, the opening in the wall, you can still see a vague outline of Machu Picchu … the dream. Although a bit fuzzy, it's still there."

"You're right, Mark. I had a lot of things I wanted to do in my life, but living got in the way of doing."

"How's that, Joseph?"

"I responded to other people's expectations of me. I put aside my youthful desires and made the choice to grow up. You know, become responsible and all that stuff."

We studied my drawing for a long moment and got lost in the realization that we had both made decisions that strayed from our dreams. I looked at my watch, drained my glass and thanked Joseph for his insight.

"Tonight, I am headed for my fiftieth reunion party. I'll bet some of my former classmates actually pursued their childhood dreams, and I intend to discover who they are and how they did it."

"That could be interesting."

"You bet! I wonder if these people have anything in common or some unique passion that helped them expand the opening in their comfort zone and escape through it."

"Tell me if anyone found their Machu Picchu," Joseph called after me.

"Gladly."

Filled with my new insight, I stepped out into the pleasant September evening and asked the concierge to call a taxi to transport me to the reception.

"Right away, sir. One is already on its way for the gentleman standing behind you."

I turned around and asked him if we could share the cab. He agreed, and we engaged in small talk about the hotel, the reunion and the weather. I had no idea who he was until I asked his name.

"Cal Patterson."

"Calvin Patterson? You were in my homeroom."

"Yes, but who are …? Oh, it's you, Mark Pierce. It's been ages."

"Only fifty years," I said. "I would never have recognized you. Something about you seems different."

"What do you mean, Mark?"

"When I knew you in high school, you were always this uptight, nervous guy — determined to make lots of money. You seem a lot different — more relaxed. Not the guy in high school."

Cal smiled and extended his hand in pleasant greeting. "My life shifted from what I was becoming to what I always wanted it to be. It took me awhile to discover my goal."

Just then, the cab pulled up, and I slipped the concierge a couple of bucks. "Let's talk on the way over to the Carleton hotel. You can tell me your story, Cal."

The cab driver worked the vehicle into traffic, and the two of us sat in the back seat. I looked at Cal, and he began his tale. "After graduating from college, I worked in the home mortgage department for First Federal Bank of Chicago. I made good money, enough to afford a place in the Marina Towers, drive a Mercedes, wear custom-made suits and enjoy an office on the twenty-fifth floor of the Prudential Building. Life unfolded just like I planned in high school. I wanted to accumulate a lot of income, retire early and, perhaps, volunteer some of my time. Yet the more I stayed in the system, the more money I made, and I got used to the opulence."

"Making a lot of money is a good thing."

"Yeah, but I never felt personally satisfied."

"Why not? You had accumulated all of those things you talked about in high school."

"But, I knew something was missing. At first, I thought I needed a relationship in my life and jumped into the dating scene, but that didn't solve anything. I searched for answers, but none came until I met Jesse. As our relationship turned into love, I realized my attraction to her came from her sense of inner peace and joy, not just her outside beauty."

"So, like most of us in the seventies, you went looking for a balance between wealth and love and kept running after the illusion of happiness."

"You could say that."

"I know, my twenties seem like a blur, as well. But, what did you learn from Jesse?"

"Jesse told me she practiced Nichiren Buddhism and chanted daily to stay focused on achieving her wants and desires."

"Really! Did it work?"

"Nothing fazed her. Calm, serene and pleasant, she went about her daily life in complete harmony — no small feat during the late sixties and seventies."

"Did you become a Buddhist like her?"

"Not at first, but the more I knew her, the more tranquil she became, and the more I wanted to know how she did it."

"And?"

"One day Jesse suggested I try chanting as a way to clarify an answer for my personal search. She taught me the mantra "Nam-myoho-renge-kyo," and told me to chant and focus on my desire to discover another path. At first, chanting seemed awkward, but I began to notice subtle changes taking place in me — like some truth would soon emerge."

"You're not going to tell me you heard a voice, are you?"

"No, much more dramatic. I received the message from a dead guy."

"What? I've got to hear this one. And if it's a good story, I'll pay for the cab."

"He smiled and said, "You won't be disappointed, so grab your wallet.""

We arrived at the hotel, and I paid the cab fare. In front of the hotel, Cal and I delayed our entrance into the party to let him finish his life-changing story.

"In 1975, my brother Phillip worked as an administrator for Cook County Hospital. I went to take him to lunch one day, and he told me he had to cancel. He was shorthanded and begged me to stay to help him with a project that was scheduled in the next hour."

Cal told me he agreed, and the two brothers headed to the hospital's basement. They walked into the morgue, and Cal saw several gurneys positioned around the room. Phillip said an anatomy class from Northwestern University had scheduled time to dissect the cadavers. Three of his staff had called in sick that morning, and he needed to provide supervision for the class.

"Phillip's exact words were, 'All you have to do is walk around the room in a white coat and look official.' I agreed."

"I assume this request had something to do with your epiphany?"

"It became the turning point in my life," Cal answered. "I felt uncomfortable around dead people to begin with, but to see them dissected would take that feeling to an entirely new level. So, to settle my nerves, I walked over to the first gurney and pulled back the sheet covering a man's head."

Cal paused for a long moment, and I leaned forward to hear the rest of the story. He noticed my interest and then said, "Here's the part that's hard to believe, and I can't tell it in any simpler, straightforward terms."

"I'm up for anything. You've got my attention."

"Okay, I swear this happened exactly as I'll tell it. I lifted up the sheet and looked down at the man. Then — this is the spooky part, but I swear it's the truth — the cadaver opened his eyes and said, 'Help us live.' "

"Unbelievable. What did you do?"

"I threw the sheet over his head and jumped back. It scared the crap out of me. My brother saw me and assured me everyone in the room, except us, had died and donated their body to science. Almost in a shock, I uncovered the body again. I didn't know if the guy was really dead or not. I poked the body and felt its icy-cold skin. Phillip was correct. They guy was dead. So, I couldn't explain how he spoke to me."

"That's really weird, Cal."

"At first, I thought so, too. Then, I began looking at the experience as a sign to do something different with my life. There are no accidents in the world — just messages that require interpretation."

"How did you interpret this experience?" I said.

"After a lot of thought and chanting, I decided to quit my job and get trained as a male nurse."

"What! You gave up everything?"

"Yes, I made a radical change: gave up a six-figure income, sold my car, moved out of the Marina Towers and altered my lifestyle."

"That's an amazing shift in focus."

"Best of all, I married Jesse, and she supported me through nursing school."

"Are you pleased with that decision?"

"Absolutely. After I became a certified nurse, Jesse and I moved to Arizona where I now work at Banner Hospital doing what the cadaver requested of me: *saving lives*."

I pondered the impact of his story. He believed he heard a voice from somewhere direct him to alter his future. I looked at him and said, "Then, you've reached an unexpected Machu Picchu."

"Excuse me?" he replied.

"It's not important to explain now, but I have a story to share with Joseph when we get back to the hotel."

Cal gave me a quizzical look and we walked toward the entrance of the Carleton. He stopped at the door to talk with another former classmate, and I slipped past and headed for the registration table.

"It is good to have an end to journey toward;
but it is the journey that matters, in the end."
— Ernest Hemingway

Chapter Twelve:
In Search of a Good Story

"We do not remember days, we remember moments. The richness of life lies in memories we have forgotten."
— Cesare Pavese

I stepped into the foyer to be greeted by Sally Broomfield, one of the members of the reunion committee. She looked up at me and smiled as I found my name tag in the rows spread out in front of her.

As I pinned it to my coat, she gasped and shouted, "Mark Pierce, at first I didn't recognize you. You look so much better as an adult."

I sheepishly smiled back and nodded, thinking, *Sally has also aged gracefully.* The years had turned her hair gray, a natural choice some women make when we reach this age. Others, however, struggle with the aging process and turn to chemicals and/or cosmetic surgery to beat father time. Then, there are those of us who have taken advantage of advanced medical technology and rely on a myriad of replacement parts to retain youth. Eventually, time wins and turns us into old fogies who slip into the next decades screaming and hollering. But, for this weekend, such morbid thinking can be shelved as we celebrate our accomplishments as classmates. I thanked Sally and headed for the bar.

I walked away from the reception table and recalled a favorite memory of Sally. While in third grade, she invited several of us to her birthday party. In her basement, we played "spin the bottle," and I remember Sally Broomfield gave me my first kiss on the lips. I liked it, and the experience sent me on a lifelong quest to find more such encounters. But, at a very young age, such events only brought embarrassment. After all these years, seeing her in a different context sent a shiver down my spine. *Compared to Linda*, I thought, *the two are worlds apart.*

I ordered a Rusty Nail, stirred the ice cubes with my finger to mix in the Drambuie and scanned the room. A pair of very young-looking high school kids — student council members, I assumed — greeted people as they arrived. They probably resented playing host to a bunch of "grumpy old farts." I watched the sweet, rosy-cheeked girl smooth some invisible wrinkle on her dress and the young man fidget with his shirt collar to relieve the discomfort of an unaccustomed necktie. *Better get used to it*, I thought. *Unless you're a computer geek like Mark Zuckerberg or Bill Gates, that's what business will expect of you.*

My mind drifted back to high school days, and the thoughts played amusing games with my senses. I recalled being a wide-eyed, tenth-grade student going to a first sock hop held in the girl's gym. Every Friday night, the school sponsored a dance to keep the kids off the streets. The principal hired some emerging rock 'n roll band, and we'd gather in that vacuous arena from 7 to 10 p.m. and listen to their tunes. Several of us who had the courage to do so awkwardly attempted to try new dance steps to the emerging rock music. I recalled paying a dollar at the door and then placing my shoes along the wall with about a hundred other pairs. At the end of the evening, a miracle occurred when we all located our own shoes. In those days, conformity to style ruled social behavior and every pair looked alike.

A student council committee always decorated the bandstand with streams of crepe paper attached to strategic places around the room. It barely altered the appearance of the gym, but none of us cared. One night, the committee outdid itself by changing the bulbs to create a soft blue tone and covering all of the lights with angel hair. That night, I met Alice and walked her home. On the way, we spent some serious time making out in the park. *Another example of what Sally started,* I mused. Funny how you forget these things for years, and then an event like this triggers a wellspring of memories. *I wonder if Alice will be here tonight.* I pondered and smiled.

I noticed several people hovering around one of the tables in the corner. With my curiosity piqued, I walked over and spotted Howard Holmes in the center of the crowd. Like the old days, Howard commanded center stage at this social event. Back then, his devilish eyes, muscular body and glib tongue fascinated all of his classmates. I could see by the gathering that Howard had not changed.

He seemed to be blessed with an intuitive sense. When trouble attracted the attention of teachers or administrators, Howie utilized his uncanny ability to blend into the background and disappear. Ironically, Howard initiated most of the pranks we played back then, but nobody caught him or realized he had been the ringleader. He looked and behaved a lot like the Eddie Haskell character on *Leave It to Beaver* — syrupy sweet, innocent on the outside, but a totally devious mind inside.

One of Howard's practical jokes encouraged members of the boy's football team to carry the coach's Volkswagen Beetle to the school's third floor. The principal suspended several of the perpetrators and others landed in detention hall, but not Howie. The conspiracy's instigator escaped and remained the unknown mastermind behind the plot. The team took a vow of silence and protected their ideological hero.

Howie often ditched study hall and enjoyed two lunch periods. He'd get bored with the silence, slide out of his seat onto the floor and crawl out the side door on his stomach. Mr. Thompson, the oblivious study hall teacher, took roll and got so involved with a favorite book he never noticed Howard's body was missing.

On other days, when Howie didn't want to soil his clothes, he enjoyed an additional free period through another form of chicanery. Before the bell rang, Howard secured a library pass from Mr. Thompson, ran down the hall to the media center and handed it to the desk clerk. The clerk noted his presence in the library, and then he'd quickly move through the stacks, walk out the back door and head for the lunchroom to enjoy more social time with friends. No one ever suspected he figured out the system and fooled everyone. Now, fifty years later, here stands the charlatan surrounded by his loyal fans, telling another tale and enticing more gullible believers.

I stepped into his circle of admiring classmates and listened to the end of Howard's story. Apparently, while working in Alaska as a backcountry tour guide, he enjoyed many unique experiences that lent themselves to an exaggerated sense of grandeur.

"One of the tourists seemed to be deathly afraid of being attacked by bears," I heard him say in a dramatic tone. Howard continued, "The frightened man asked me, 'What's the best way to keep bears from mauling you when you're hiking?' I told him that it was easy. ... Just attach a couple of those little jingle bells to your shoelaces. When the bears hear that sound, they'll run away to avoid contact with humans. If you want to feel even safer, I'd recommend carrying a can of bear spray."

Former classmates pictured the scenario Howard painted and nodded in agreement. However, the crafty raconteur had not finished. He had paused long enough to keep his audience hanging on every word — just like he did as a high school student.

"Then the man asked another question about bears," Howie continued. "He had seen a lot of bear scat on hiking trails and wanted to know how you could tell the difference between scat left by black bears and the remains of grizzly bear droppings."

Howard used his impeccable sense of timing to ensure his listeners realized the depth of fear the tourist expressed. Years of exaggeration and a refined sense of stage presence provided him with a perfect penchant for the dramatic. Once he captured everyone's attention, Howard slipped in his matter-of-fact punch line.

"That's easy, I said. The scat of a black bear is usually filled with undigested berries and seeds, and it often smells like honey …." Pausing again for maximum effect, he added, "and the scat of a grizzly bear is usually filled with remnants of tiny bells, undigested shoe laces and smells a lot like bear spray!"

His classmates hooted and howled when they realized Howard's story had been a playful joke all along. The laughter subsided, and his audience splintered into groups of twos and threes — all sharing stories about fifty years of vacation memories. With a self-satisfied smile, Howard took a long swig of his drink.

The intermission gave me an opportunity to talk alone with him. "Clever story, Howie. You haven't lost your touch." He glanced in my direction. "Do you remember me? I'm Mark Pierce."

"Of course, Mark. It's been a long time. Nice to see you again."

"You, too. Mind if I ask how you ended up in Alaska after graduating from Oak Ridge?"

"No, of course not," Howard grinned. "Remember, my father was a Major in the Navy, and I was born in London.

The family moved every two years, or so, before I enrolled in Oak Ridge to finish out my high school years."

"I vaguely recall that. Must have been a hard way to grow up — make new friends and change schools so often."

"Yeah, real shitty elementary school memories," he continued, "especially when we moved in mid-year — I was always the new kid walking into a strange class with thirty sets of eyes looking at me. Right away, I got challenged by the class bully at every new school I attended. So, I avoided fighting by being funny ... became the class clown out of necessity."

"None of that sounds like much fun," I said.

"No, but it taught me to accept constant change in life. By the time I came here, I figured out how to make adjustments and survive. Life became quiet for me in Oak Ridge."

"What do you mean?" I asked.

"My dad got a four-year assignment at the naval base in Chicago, and our travels ended. I had four years in high school to make friends. The crazy pranks I played made me popular. I felt pretty cool, and it improved my ego. After graduation, Oak Ridge seemed too subdued, and I realized how much I missed discovering new and different things in the world. I wasn't ready to settle down any place for keeps."

I smiled at his insight and said, "Your search for a Machu Picchu sent you spinning around the world looking for adventure."

"Not Machu Picchu. I haven't visited any Inca cities yet. But, I have been to a lot of wonderful places ... *out there*." His hand gesture almost knocked the Rusty Nail out of my hand, and I had to steady the plastic cup with the other. My reference to Machu Picchu got lost in the commotion, and I didn't try to explain.

"What did you do to escape from Oak Ridge? How did you achieve your dream of exploring ... out there?" I made a sweeping motion with my free hand to mimic his gesture and turned sideways to protect my drink.

"After graduation, Dad pulled a few strings and got me an appointment to West Point. God, what a mistake. With all that pomp, tradition and soldier-boy discipline, I lasted six weeks — quit school and headed to New York City where I became a dock worker."

"Then what?"

"I got a job as a deckhand on a freighter that took me back to London. I transferred to other boats headed for destinations throughout Europe and ended up in Italy. By chance, I ran into a guy in an Italian bar who needed an additional crew member on a sailing ship that catered to tourists. That job changed my life."

"How?"

When I was a student at Oak Ridge High, I loved studying world history, especially ancient Greece, Rome and Egypt. While on the tourist ship, I started sharing the stories Mr. Atkins, our old world history teacher, used to tell in class. Remember, he shared accounts about people's lives and their personal screw-ups. I loved going to history just to hear him talk about the secret sex lives of the ancients. For me, they became real people. The history books seemed so dry, but Atkins added a personal flare to the subject. So, after high school, I read more stories about historical characters and became a great storyteller and shipboard hero."

"You owe your success to old Mr. Atkins?"

"Once I started telling those stories and adding my own twist to them, I developed a following among every group of tourists. They asked me to be their personal tour guide whenever we docked at a port ... and they tipped me well."

"So, the ship captain recognized your skill and promoted you?"

"Precisely." Howard slapped me on the back, causing me the spill the last of my drink. "My ability to tell stories got me promoted from deckhand to travel guide. People recognized my passion for adventure and ability to turn legends into believable tales. I easily transitioned into a new career."

"So, how did you end up in Alaska?" I asked, returning to my original question.

"The captain started his own adventure-bound tour company and offered me a job. I did so well I soon became a partner in the business."

"That's fortunate," I added.

"The best part of becoming a modern explorer means you always have an adoring audience in tow, willing to pay for their entertainment. I guided tours to Egypt, Africa, the Amazon River and the remote jungles of India, and explored the outback of Australia and didn't put out any of my own money. In fact, the tourists paid my way. I finally started my own company and ended up in the glacier fields of Alaska. I've been there for the past six years."

"Your travel escapades turned your dream into a well-paying business," I responded.

"Right you are, Mark. I owe it all to the quiet, sedate life here in Oak Ridge. My time in high school taught me what I didn't want. My experiences as a military brat instilled a wandering spirit in my being. I recognized the entire world was an adventure waiting for me to embrace, ... and I've done it all with gusto and flare for the past fifty years."

Richard Case and his wife interrupted our conversation. "Howard, Howard, ... I've been looking all over for you. Please tell my wife how you had to wrestle that anaconda in South America. It's such a fascinating story. Oh, excuse me," he said looking in my direction, "I didn't mean to interrupt." Richard didn't recognize me, and I didn't want to surprise him.

"No problem, I need another drink." I looked into my empty glass and added, "Howard, thanks for the story. I'll see you later."

He nodded and turned to his newly acquired, audience.

On my way back to the bar, I noticed three large men staring at me. They looked like former football players, but I didn't recognize any of them. One of them raised two fingers to his eyes mimicking the Robert De Niro "I'm watching you" gesture. I almost laughed, but felt a shiver of fear run up my back. *Were these guys threatening to beat me up or something?* I thought. *Did Judy tell them to get me? Grow up guys.*

"Mark, get a grip, man," I said to my empty glass. "You're being a bit paranoid, aren't you?" I shook my head and walked to the bar for another cocktail. The oversized adolescents maintained their vigil and watched me from a distance.

> "Live the full life of the mind, exhilarated by new ideas, intoxicated by the romance of the unusual."
> — Ernest Hemingway

Chapter Thirteen:
Blindsided by Rage

"Let us not look back in anger, nor forward in fear, but around in awareness."
— James Thurber

I blended the Drambuie and scotch with a stir stick and reflected on Howie's life. *The grand manipulator, the party boy, the class clown leaves his adoring followers in Oak Ridge in search of his vision of happiness and emerges as a folk hero, a role model for his clients. Who would have predicted that? With all of the schemes he concocted in high school, it's no wonder he could help people explore their own fantasies. Howie's got the kind of personality that moves him to the top of the "must invite" list at parties.*

I chuckled at my observation, took a sip of my drink and looked around the room for other people I knew. My gaze was drawn to an irritated couple headed in my direction. Red-faced, it looked as if the woman intended to thrash me. She did. Within an arm's length, she slapped my face with her right hand, sending my drink flying across the floor. The unexpected disturbance silenced the guests standing in the vicinity.

"That's for Ruth Ann, you bastard," she fumed. "You have a lot of nerve coming back here, Mark Pierce. You robbed Ruthie of her future. I hate you. You think you can just traipse into our gathering and pretend we forgot? You should have gone to jail."

My face stung, and I could feel a welt rising on my cheek. I stepped back, rubbed my face and looked at her in shock. I didn't know how to respond.

The woman's husband grabbed her arms and pinned them to her side.

Suddenly, I felt nauseous and gripped my stomach. I looked at the faces of bystanders staring in my direction. Reality had thrown me a sucker punch, and it landed squarely on target. For months, I had dreaded experiencing this kind of confrontation, and now it happened. *At last*, I thought, *someone has finally broken the social boundaries and acted on their pent-up feelings.*

The woman struggled to free herself from her husband's grip, and my memory of them flashed in my mind.

Ron Stevens and Mary Ackerman dated throughout high school. They loved being known as the cutest couple on campus. He played on the basketball, football and baseball teams, and she pretended to be a cheerleader. They rode on the same athletic bus to all of his events and sat in the last seat, known as the passion pit, and made out like crazy. Inevitably, Mary got pregnant and spent her senior year in Iowa. Ron joined her after graduation, and they got married in a simple ceremony on a farm outside Cedar Rapids. The following year, Ron, Mary and Chad, their new son, returned to Oak Ridge to become partners in his family's furniture business.

Mary, one of those babbling bathroom babes, talked about everyone and everything in school — an early vitriolic gossip-monger who enjoyed being the center of attention. Her social status in high school relied on her ability to be the first one to spread juicy stories. Emerging from bathroom smoke breaks with other cunning cuties, she pretended to be the town crier. Her rumors caused tidal waves of indignant gossip that cascaded through the halls like a spring runoff, disrupting the school's social scene and drenching all in its path. Mary played the role of the main stalk in the school's grapevine.

Like Judy, Mary would now accelerate the news of my presence to the rest of Oak Ridge. Her former popularity anointed her with the power to get what she wanted, and now she wanted my hide. *Of all the people to run into*, I thought, *why Mary?*

Ron strengthened his grip on his wife and tried to strategically position himself between the two of us to avoid a bigger scene. "Mary's right, Mark. What are you doing here?" he said.

Age had not been kind to the pair. Their former athletic frames had turned pear-shaped, probably from excessive eating and sedentary behaviors. The retired cheerleader's face once filled with vibrancy, now revealed deep lines and creases — a living testament to years of scowling and anger. Ron's formerly bushy head of hair had all but disappeared, and it looked as if the typical male-pattern balding did its worst damage to him as a young man. Rather than settle for the "cul-de-sac look" with a line of hair around his ears, Ron decided to shave it all off and present the world with his version of an "open space concept." Even under the lights of the reception room, his head glistened like a polished cue ball.

My mind snapped back to the moment as I heard Mary's grating voice shout at me again. "Well, well, ... what do you have to say for yourself?" She peppered me with a spray of saliva. "If I were a man, I'd take you outside and whip your ass."

She broke her husband's grip and stood toe-to-toe with me. I watched her plump arms fold over a drooping chest.

She impatiently tapped a foot on the floor, waiting for a response.

Shocked by her aggressive behavior, I took a step back and prepared for another assault. The tension made my mind go numb.

I couldn't think, so only nodded and said, "Ron? Mary?"

Again, she snapped at me, "We're not here to make pleasant conversation, Mark. Why don't you go back to where you came from and leave us alone. Haven't you figured out we don't want you here?" Her glare intensified.

Finally, I said, "I wanted ... to heal old wounds ... fifty years is a long time."

"Not ... long ... enough," she bit off each syllable. "Listen to me, Mister ... Mark ... Pierce. People in this town will never forgive you, ... understand? This is *not* the time nor the place to get a pardon from any of us. It's not ever going to happen. You ruined lives."

Again, Ron grabbed Mary by the arms, attempting to pull her away. He looked at me with pleading eyes. "Have you talked with any of them yet?"

"No, Ron. I just got here last night. I thought the reunion would be the best place to deal with it because everyone would be here ...." I hesitated. "But, I guess I was wrong."

Mary tore loose from her husband's grip a second time and verbally lashed at me again. "If I were any of them, I'd rather shoot you. There's nothing you can say to change what happened or to take away the pain of that night."

"Look, Mary," I yelled, "I know there are no "do overs" in life, but after all this time, it's important for me to apologize and find forgiveness."

"If you ask me, it's too little and much too late for any of that. I'd rather spit on you, than forgive you. Do us a favor. Go away. Get out. Don't spoil this party like you did our graduation."

I snipped back. "You weren't even there that night. It must have killed you to have been way out in Iowa … too difficult to gossip from that distance."

My comment made her more furious, as Ron griped his agitated, slightly inebriated wife again. "Mary, really, it's none of our business. It's over. Let Mark deal with his own ghosts." Looking at me, he said, "Please leave, Mark. This is too upsetting for everyone."

Ron pulled her away, and Mary looked back at me. "I only hope you feel as much pain as you dished out."

Then, Ron led her into another room. People who stood by watching and listening averted their eyes and went on with their conversations. Completely shaken, I asked the bartender for a double scotch, straight up, and a small glass of ice. My cheek felt like it was on fire. I'm sure I had a red handprint embossed on my face. I downed the double and headed out a side door into the hotel's garden with melting ice cubes tightly pressed to my face.

"The only thing that could spoil a day was people. People were always the limiters of happiness except for the very few that were as good as spring itself."
— Ernest Hemingway

Chapter Fourteen: Words of Wisdom

"Intelligence is quickness in seeing things as they are."
— George Santayana

Heart pounding rapidly and hands shaking; I knew it would only be a matter of time before someone like Mary confronted me again. My reaction to her encounter surprised me. Perspiration soaked my new shirt, and I felt like throwing up. An unfamiliar feeling of panic consumed my mind, and I berated myself for thinking the trip would solve anything.

I paced the dimly lit garden and noticed someone lighting a cigarette under a tree. I walked past the smoker, and a hand unexpectedly emerged from the shadows to offer me a drag. The voice said, "I know you never smoked in high school, but this may be of help now."

I took it and inhaled deeply. I stepped closer and recognized another classmate. The stoic face of Wesley Reasoner moved into the light where I could see him better. "Thanks, Wesley," I uttered, handing the smoke back to him. He held up a hand and said, "Keep it. He lit another and drew in a puff. I heard Mary's irritating voice all the way out here."

"You don't remember me, do you, Wesley?"

"Vaguely ... just your reputation. You and I never had classes together." Wesley studied my face and added, "I'm surprised you know who I am."

"You," I said. "None of us actually knew *you*, but we recognized your brain power and that fact alone intimidated most of us." I inhaled again and the additional nicotine settled my nerves. "I'm Mark Pierce."

"Based on the scene Mary created inside, I figured it out. Finally caught up to you, didn't it?"

"Yes, and in a public gathering, as well." I took another drag on the cigarette, trying to find words to say to this stranger. "Enough about my uncomfortable past. ... Why are you out here in the garden?"

Wesley snuffed out his cigarette in a flower urn next to him and responded, "I was never one to socialize in formal settings. Besides, gardening has become a passion of mine, and I take every opportunity to be with some of my closest living friends — plants."

"Yeah, I remember *you never played well with others*," mocking the trite phrase teachers put on our report cards in elementary school. "God, your brain put you way above the rest of us mortals at school. Why would you ever want to play with us anyway?"

"Small chitchat and sports talk always made me uncomfortable," he said. "I never knew what to say without sounding stupid. So, I took refuge in reading books about Einstein, philosophy or the Renaissance Masters."

"I used to watch you in the halls," I said, "lost in thought or reading a book as you walked, oblivious to your surroundings, like you were trying to figure out some scientific formula."

"Right, I was always distracted by ideas and avoided eye contact because I had so many interesting thoughts racing through my head. My lack of social skills, made me feel shy and awkward, and I took refuge within myself."

"We all thought you were a bit nerdy, but never criticized your amazing intelligence. I remember the story about how you once used all three chalkboards in Mr. Ryan's advanced calculus class to show the proof for one of his challenge problems. I wasn't smart enough to take calculus, but I heard you astounded all the students in class with that move, and your fame spread throughout the school."

Wesley smiled and said, "Yeah, I do remember that A.P. calc class. Mr. Ryan told me I got the right answer, but my messy work needed improvement. His discipline and strict approach to solving math problems played a big part of my future career."

"What did you end up doing?" I asked.

"I became a chemical engineer and now own a few patents, but never won the Pulitzer Prize in science," he joked.

"Where did you go after high school?" I asked.

"I got a full-ride scholarship to the University of Michigan, then another free ride at M.I.T. I finally ended up at Harvard University and earned my Ph.D. in chemistry. I always said I'd make it to the Ivy League. Became a full professor there, spent most of my career teaching at a university in the east and then took a research position in Texas."

"Sounds like a pretty fantastic life, *Dr. Reasoner*," I said in amazement. "Ever have any thoughts about returning to Oak Ridge?"

"No, Oak Ridge gave me a good high school education, but I never felt intellectually challenged by teachers or friends here." He paused and reflected, "With all due respect for our school, I missed having intense discussions about books and concepts that were virtually unknown to many of my classmates at Oak Ridge."

"Are you saying we weren't smart enough for you?" I pressed.

"No, no, Mark. That sounds far too arrogant for me and smacks of intellectual snobbery. That doesn't match my personality, because I never felt superior." He paused as if he searched for the words to help me understand his thoughts. "You see," he began, "my parents encouraged me to read as soon as I learned the alphabet. By the time I was in junior high school, I had read Plato, Socrates and much of Shakespeare's work. My parents talked with me about books all the time. They instilled in me an intense intellectual curiosity and desire to explore ideas and possibilities."

"Growing up in your family must have made you feel pretty special."

"Yes, I enjoyed the attention of being an only child, but felt isolated and alone ... no real friends."

"Then, finding intellectual camaraderie motivated you to leave Oak Ridge?"

"You could say that. I had a thirst to surround myself with kindred spirits — minds that had a passion to explore the unknown. I yearned to be in an intellectual environment where colleagues investigated the connections between acceptable theories and unproven notions. I desired to have the challenge of combining ideas in unique ways. I couldn't find it here."

"But, you eventually found it in the Ivy League schools."

"Yes, nothing negative intended about Oak Ridge, but the more I stayed in the east, the more satisfied I felt."

I watched the excitement in Wesley's eyes as his story rekindled the enthusiasm of his chosen path.

"People who ignored personal criticism and had the courage to take a risk attracted me. They put their professional reputation on the line all the time and sometimes failed — knowing that process was more important than the product."

"Risk-takers," I smiled. "You've become a risk-taker — the kind of person who will stick a finger into a dark hole looking for the answer to an unknown mystery and unafraid something may bite it off."

Wesley chuckled, drained his beer and told me he needed another drink. I thanked him for his honesty and shook his hand. Before stepping back into the reception, he stopped to add another insight.

"You know, Mark," he smiled, "I didn't stay in my intellectual cocoon forever. I matured with age. I expanded my interests. I now grow exotic plants, play the bass in a jazz band and prepare some mean gourmet recipes. I even adopted some negative habits, like smoking a pack a day, and I learned how to distill my own liquor. I'm like the guy in the *Dos Equis* commercials. He's suave and sophisticated with women, well-traveled and a bit mysterious." He grinned at me. "Over the years, I've done a first-rate job of balancing my intellect with the joys of the good life."

I laughed and said, "Wesley, I bet you have." I saluted him with two fingers as he disappeared inside.

I compared my post-high school adventure to Wesley's life. *The biggest difference in our two experiences, besides the huge spread in IQ scores,* I thought, *centered on our motivation to leave Oak Ridge. Wesley ran toward his dreams, explored intellectual curiosity and spent the next fifty years with colleagues who nurtured and encouraged him. He found Machu Picchu in his mind, and I continue to live with doubts because I ran and hid from my dreams.*

Alone again, I took a deep breath and ran my fingers along the side of my face. It still burned. The conversation with Wesley gave me a chance to calm down and let the cooling properties of the ice work its magic. I started to return to the reception when I spotted the three enforcers standing by the garden door. One smacked his right fist into his cupped left hand in a threatening gesture. He didn't see me in the dark, but that sickening feeling returned, and I felt trapped by spiteful classmates.

Really? Threats of violence at my age? I wonder if this is what the nerds of our generation experienced when they were confronted by the school bullies? I thought. *I've had enough of this for one night. I'll head out the back and call it an evening.*

> "Happiness in intelligent people
> is the rarest thing I know."
> — Ernest Hemingway

Chapter Fifteen:
Adjusting to Reality

"There is love of course. And then there's life, its enemy."
— Jean Anouilh

I slipped out the garden gate, walked to the front of the hotel and hailed a cab. The driver's eyes appeared in the rearview mirror and asked, "Where to, mister?"

"Oak Ridge Inn, please." The cab drove off, and I peered into the darkened streets, trying to make sense of the evening.

"Excuse me, sir," the driver said, invading my disconnected daze, "I think I should know you."

"A lot of people mistake me for an actor," I said, "but I'm not."

"No, I never thought you resembled any actor I know, but somehow you do look familiar."

"I don't live here — used to — just visiting from San Francisco," I responded in a flat, distant tone. I had no desire to make small talk with a cabbie and yearned to get into bed.

"Were you at the Oak Ridge reception tonight?"

"Yes, I graduated from Oak Ridge with the class of '61."

"Me, too," his voice perked up. "Then we must have been classmates. I'm Curtis Cunningham," he smiled, turned and looked at me over his right shoulder.

"Curtis!" I shouted. "I just saw your eyes and the back of your head. What the hell are you doing driving a cab? I figured you would have been a famous artist by now. Why weren't you at the reunion tonight?"

"I'll be there tomorrow. The cab driving thing's another story." He hesitated. "I think I remember your name. ... It's Mark something, isn't it?"

"Good memory, Curtis. Mark Pierce."

"No, I cheated. Several people already know you're back and don't like it."

"Oh, fine," I said. "I've been here one day, and even a cab driver knows my whereabouts." I joked, "In high school, nobody voted me 'most popular,' and I don't have to worry about winning that honor now."

Curtis tactfully changed the subject. "Plan to stay long after the reunion, Mark?"

"No, I'll head back to San Francisco on Monday."

Curtis handed me a card with his name on it. "Give me a call on Monday morning, and I'll drive you back to the airport."

"Thanks, Curtis, I will." I shoved his business card in my coat pocket and asked, "You have to explain why you're driving a cab."

"Tell you what, you're my last fare tonight. When we get to the hotel, I'll buy you a drink and fill you in."

"Curtis, if you're a storyteller, I'll buy the drinks. It will probably offer you a bigger tip, anyway."

"You're on, Mark."

For the remainder of the ride, Curtis and I reminisced about teachers, athletic teams, dances and classes we shared. Fifteen minutes later, we sat in the hotel bar nursing drinks and munching on a bowl of pretzels. Joseph had been replaced by another bartender, and my Machu Picchu stories would have to wait for his return. Now I concentrated on Curtis.

"A cab driver? That's the last thing I ever pictured you doing. With your artistic talent, I thought you'd become a graphic artist or something. What happened?"

"Lots of unexpected events changed the future. My parents gave me a small college fund, enough to enroll in the arts program at the community college. I worked part-time as a furniture mover — flexible hours and good money, probably too good. I stayed in that job too long — more than a decade — and lost my interest in art.

"From personal experience, I know it's easy to slip off the path when you least expect it," I said.

"Then I met Cynthia, eight years younger than me, and the most beautiful woman I'd ever seen. Even though she referred to me as "her old man," we fell madly in love and got married within a year."

"Curtis, I remember you as a quiet guy who planned out life and relished your art work. Your diversion surprises me," I interrupted.

"Yeah, that was true about the old Curtis, but Cynthia turned the new Curtis into a delighted pile of mush. Consumed with passion, we used to go to the park at night and lie in the grass and watch the stars. Listening to her heart beat and watching her profile in the moonlight brought me sheer contentment. I spent hours in her presence, and she distracted my pursuit of art, but I never regretted it."

"Wow, I once read there are three images one never forgets: the sight of a majestic mountain, watching a man ride a camel and seeing a man in love. Even now, you sparkle with still being in love. It must have been pure bliss."

"Totally consuming. Both Cynthia and I quit school, moved into an apartment we fixed up in my parent's basement, and got hourly jobs to pay for essentials — lived, loved and played as another decade slipped away." His eyes glistened as he recalled those joyous times.

We ordered another round of drinks, and then I watched the color disappear from his face.

"Cynthia and I were very cautious with our lovemaking — no room for a child. Then, the unexpected happened: We slipped up, and she got pregnant. I guess you can't spend that much time making passionate love and expect to keep it all to yourself, can you?"

I shrugged in ignorance, because I had no clue about that kind of intensity or depth of love. I couldn't relate. The more he spoke about his life with Cynthia, the more I envied him. *I spent a great deal of time running away from my feelings and didn't plunge into love like he did, even when I got married and had kids,* I thought.

Curtis continued. "Justin, my son, became such a happy baby, grinning at everyone and everything. He loved to be held and cuddled and, from the very beginning, mesmerized his grandparents and our friends. Without a doubt, Justin was the perfect child, being nurtured in the most loving environment possible."

"I looked at my former classmate and said, "You must have been one of the most fortunate men alive — to have such a passionate, romantic connection at that age and then blessed with a beautiful child."

"Yes, God and the entire universe smiled on our good fortune. I set aside some money and started back to art school. Things began to look up, and I got on track to pursue my career again." After finishing the sentence, his body went silent, grew dark. Finally, he looked at me with a somber expression and said, "Then, life turned tragic."

I saw tears welling up in his eyes. One by one, they trickled down his cheeks. He took a long drink and composed his thoughts. He had more to share and wanted to push through the emotional veil that clouded his thinking. I silently waited.

"One weekend, Cynthia and I decided to head for the Wisconsin Dells for some alone time. Mom and Dad volunteered to take care of ten-year-old Justin. We left after tucking Justin in bed and drove north on the interstate toward Wisconsin. Rush hour had ended, and we made good time. Then, without warning, it happened." He paused again and struggled to speak the next sentence. "I had no time to react."

"To what?" I leaned forward to hear his softly spoken words.

Curtis took a deep breath and began to stumble his way through the explanation. "I was going the speed limit ... in the right lane ... following all the rules." He paused again.

Reliving the moment now filled his eyes with more tears, and the words came slowly, measured by a painful memory. He released a heavy sigh and explained, "A car with no lights ... stalled in the lane just ahead of us. The driver forgot to turn on his emergency flashers. ... I never saw it ... too dark, too dark. A small rise in the road obscured my view. I couldn't swerve out of the way and rear-ended his car going sixty-five miles an hour."

"Oh, my god," I said and placed my hand on his back.

Streams of tears flowed down his cheeks. He took several breaths before continuing. "Just before we came up to the stalled vehicle, Cynthia took off her seatbelt to search for something in the back seat. On impact, her body went through the front windshield and landed fifty yards away. They said she died instantly."

He wept in silence as I continued to rub his back.

"I wasn't that lucky. The force of the impact shattered both my legs. The ambulance crew had to put parts of my leg bones in a plastic sack and bring them to the hospital on the stretcher with me. My hips were broken in two places, and I had glass shards embedded in my face and chest. Over the next year, I had more than a dozen operations as they tried to piece me together."

"How terrible. Survival can sometimes be worse than death," I mumbled.

"Yeah, I sat in a wheelchair for almost a year and now live on disability. I still have steel pins and a couple of rods holding my legs together and have trouble walking or standing for any length of time."

"What happened to the people in the other car?" I asked.

"Nothing. They were standing on the side of the road and were fine. Ironically, the guy had no insurance and a suspended license. He got some consequences, but he still gets to walk around, and his family is still alive."

"What happened after the accident?" A hundred questions flooded my mind, but I wanted to let Curtis tell me only what he chose to share.

"Initially, I stayed with my parents, and they helped me raise Justin. When I started walking again, I got a job as the manager of a UPS store, but had to quit because the cement floors made the pain unbearable. I refused to take mind-numbing drugs to get through the day because I wanted to stay alert so I could raise my son."

"But, Curtis, you still had your talent — your artistic skill. Couldn't you have gone back to school, or moved to New York or Chicago for a job?" I ran off a series of questions in a staccato-like fashion. "As a graphic artist, you could have done all of your work sitting down."

Curtis looked at me with a resigned expression and explained, "No, my main job was to raise Justin. Besides, all the bills killed me, and insurance benefits for the accident ran out, leaving me with no money to finish art school."

"You must have felt confined," I said.

"Confined? Hell, no. Raising Justin became the most important job of my life. It's what Cynthia would have wanted."

Curtis grew silent and ordered another drink. We both studied the melting ice in our glasses, and then he continued,

"Leaving Oak Ridge was never an option. Our tragedy made it more important to stay close to the support of family, friends and Justin's school. Without his mother's presence, he needed stability in his life more than ever. We lived in the same house until he finished school. I still live there. Justin had friends he could count on. I tried to make life as normal as possible without his mom. Until he graduated from high school, his grandparents and I were always there for him."

"And ... your dreams, Curtis?"

"They went on hold ... forever. I had enough money coming in from disability and part-time jobs to pay the bills, but not enough for my schooling. I decided to save for Justin's future. I never regretted the choice I made."

"And what happened to your son?" I asked.

"He graduated from high school and got a scholarship to attend the Chicago Art Institute. Unlike me, his fascination with computers turned him into a wonderful graphic artist. He's married, and they live downtown. His wife's a school teacher and loves Justin very much. I'm happy for them."

I finished my Rusty Nail and signaled the bartender for another. He brought Curtis another drink and announced last call — perfect timing for me. I had passed my limit and craved sleep. Operating on emotional overload for the past six hours, I had to shut down. I finished my drink and, uncharacteristically, gave Curtis a hug and told him I'd see him at the dinner tomorrow. He planned to leave his cab at home for the next couple of days and celebrate with our former classmates.

"Hey, Curtis. Look for me tomorrow night. I hear there's safety in numbers, and I may need some support."

"I'll be there for you, Mark."

I headed for my room, too tired to analyze anything else. In a matter of minutes, I crashed in bed. I thought about Curtis and felt lucky to have Linda in my life. *I need to tell her that*, I thought and drifted into a deep, sound sleep.

"There is no lonelier man in death, except the suicide, than that man who has lived many years with a good wife and then outlived her. If two people love each other there can be no happy end to it."
— Ernest Hemingway

Chapter Sixteen:
Out of the Shadows

"The truth is that our finest moments are most likely to occur when we are feeling deeply uncomfortable, unhappy, or unfulfilled. For it is only in such moments, propelled by our discomfort, that we are likely to step out of our ruts and start searching for different ways or truer answers."
— M. Scott Peck

I woke early, feeling intense hunger. The lack of dinner, supplemented by a small bowl of pretzels, failed to offset the dose of reality I swallowed at the reception. I showered before room service delivered a huge breakfast and ravenously downed everything on the tray. I tried to record my thoughts from the previous day in my notebook, but the words came out in a jumbled mess. My presence here created a drama that rattled my thinking and gnawed at my senses like some ensnared animal. I refocused and wrote:

> *I never talked about it with anyone. I ran away like a coward and buried my feelings. The images have festered in people's minds for years. Unresolved events almost got me beaten up last night. The folks who stayed in Oak Ridge had to deal with their anger and never knew the truth. I accept the blame. It's time to confront a new reality.*

I got stuck while many others moved on to confront real life issues. Curtis sacrificed his dream and became a dedicated parent who nurtured his son and used family and the Oak Ridge community to get through loss. They filled the void left by Cynthia's untimely death. The dark hole I left remained empty, filled only with shadows and questions. *Stop being a coward, Mark,* I thought. *Time to put things right, no matter what the cost.*

I paced the room, trying to determine my next move. The homecoming game, scheduled for noon, offered a small window of opportunity to act on my feelings. I shuddered to think I could be accosted again in public or chewed out by another angry classmate. I had to do something this morning. I located the name in the local telephone directory and called from the room.

"Hello," the pleasant voice spoke into the phone.

After all these years, I recognized it. "Hello, Carol, this is Mark Pierce," I said and held my breath.

The line went still, and I could barely hear her breathing. It seemed like a long time before Carol responded, "I heard you finally came back into town."

"Probably from Judy, I bet."

"No, I got the message from another source further down the line."

"Yeah, but I'm sure Judy set off the original alarm."

It was always like that with Carol, I thought. *We'd have these little pitiful disagreements about the smallest things that distracted us from what was important. But, it happened every time. ... Why did I always get sucked into this mundane banter with her?*

"Why are you calling me?" she asked, interrupting my thoughts.

"I need to talk with you," I pleaded.

"You needed to talk with me fifty years ago — in June of 1961, only ...," she paused, "only you decided to run away and not even say goodbye. Six months later, I get a crummy card from someplace in Sweden saying, 'I'm sorry.' Mark, it was not enough then, and it's ... too late now."

"I was afraid to talk with you back then. I was confused, disoriented on pain meds. But, believe me, the past is what I need to talk with you about," I implored.

"Nothing you say or do will change things. What happened is old news, over, gone, ... and most of us have spent our adult lives trying to get past it."

"I'm sorry, Carol. ... I was ... no, I am such a slow learner — never good at sharing my feelings. You, of all people, know that. For the last five decades, I tried to hide from the truth ... to swallow it, but I can't do that anymore. The reunion offered me a chance to clear things up and that's why I came back. I've got to start with you. I hurt lots of people, and I thought those terrible feelings would go away, but they haven't."

Silence filled the space that linked our two phones like an invisible lifeline ... some magical fiber-optic cable barely holding us together. I remained quiet and listened to her breathing. I wanted my words to sink in and make sense. I waited, then waited some more. Finally, I heard her inhale. It sounded like she was on the verge of crying. I listened more intensely, hoping for the response I wanted ... needed to hear.

"You know, Mark, I loved you so deeply. We talked about getting married. You abandoned me."

Her voice trailed off as she sniffed. I sat listening, waiting, giving her an opportunity to speak the words she must have rehearsed for years before giving up on me. When she spoke again, I could tell the tears stored away for so long were now being released.

"Mark, I loved you, and then I hated you for the pain you brought us. You and I were so stupid. Some of us have never fully recovered. Don't you understand how many lives were ruined?"

"I know, I know, Carol. I'm sorry. I couldn't face you or talk about it. I felt the pain and anger at the graduation ceremony. I was devastated and had to run ... hide ... forget."

"You did a great job of hiding, Mark. I don't understand why you bothered to come back at all. Are you trying to rub it in now?"

"No, Carol, I came back because I need to uncover answers, seek forgiveness — discover a way to pardon myself and find a way to achieve peace with you."

"You may be in for a long, disappointing weekend," she said.

"The only thing I have left is to express my sorrow to each of you I hurt and ask you to forgive my childhood mistake. If you're not ready to grant me that much, I'll understand, but I had to start somewhere. You were my closest friend."

"It's pretty gutsy of you to call me, because your behavior got you into this mess in the first place, didn't it?"

"Carol, is there any way I can see you for coffee or a drink while I'm here? It's pretty awkward talking on the phone. I'm much better in person."

"God, Mark. You're asking an awful lot of me."

"I know, but I need to talk with you — to understand. We shared something ... once. I'm asking you ... please, do this as a favor for an old ... lost friend."

"Oh, shit! I'm such a soft touch. Okay, let's meet after the homecoming game at Red's Lounge on Marion and Lake Street."

"Thank you, Carol. Say about 4 p.m.?"

"Just a short one. I've got to get dolled up for the reunion dinner and dance at the Oak Ridge Country Club tonight."

"I'll be there." Now it was my turn to fight off a wellspring of emotions and stumble over my words. "Thank you ... again ... for granting me this favor." My eyes overflowed, and I could say no more.

"See you after the game, Mark."

> "When you start to live outside yourself,
> it's all dangerous."
> — Ernest Hemingway

Chapter Seventeen: Voices in the Stands

"To look backward for a while,
is to refresh the eye to restore it,
and to render it the more fit for
its prime function of looking forward."
— Margaret Fairless Barber

I arrived at the football stadium as the gates opened. I purchased an obligatory set of orange and blue pom-poms, our school colors, and a Class of '61 alumni pin. A cheerful, petite cheerleader, acting as a docent for the alumni, guided me to the special homecoming section near the fifty-yard line. I asked directions to the concession stand to purchase a hot dog and Coke. Heeding the call of nature, I also located the nearest washroom. The cheerleader, who pointed me in the right direction, gave me a motherly pat on the arm and danced away. *Ah, youth*, I thought, *how innocent, how lucky, how unencumbered by mistakes.*

I located a seat in the highest corner of the stadium so I could secretly observe the arrival of my former classmates. *From this vantage point,* I thought, *I can choose the people I want to talk with and avoid unwanted confrontations.*

To pass the time, I opened the alumni packet and read the facts about the Class of '61. More than eight hundred students graduated. The alumni association tracked down almost all of them. Sadly, I discovered nearly a quarter of our class died before they reached this milestone celebration — the first while we were still in school and the last only a few months ago. I looked at the number and pondered their fate. *Had they accomplished their life goals before death took them? Did they find love and happiness?*

Another set of statistics caught my attention to dislodge my maudlin thoughts. Almost forty percent of my former classmates still lived within a fifty-mile radius of Oak Ridge, and another thirty-eight percent live outside the area. Too bad I couldn't tell if they had recently retired and moved to warmer climates, or if they left shortly after high school to pursue a job, go to college or be with a spouse. If I had the time, I could check that out, but I came for a different, more important personal mission. My comfort zone theory would have to wait and evolve in its own time.

Our class graduated just before the Vietnam War heated up. More than twenty-five percent of our class served in a branch of the military — some even made the service a career. I knew Oak Ridge had the reputation for being a fine academic high school, but I never realized almost thirty-eight percent of our graduating class went to college, another five percent completed advanced degrees and a handful more earned doctorates. That may have been a trend of the early 1960s, but sitting in the stands fifty years later, I sense a new appreciation for the kind of education I took for granted as a goofy seventeen-year-old.

The brochure also listed the occupations we entered after graduating. I scanned the categories, and some of the personal success stories impressed me. People found a variety of traditional and innovative ways to earn a living and achieve lifelong dreams. I glanced through a list of names and recognized many of my classmates who became teachers, entered government service, started their own businesses or joined the medical profession. Still other names listed career choices in finance, marketing, advertising, religion, law, and many more. *Who would have thought my former friends and classmates could do so many diverse things.*

Unaware of our place in the world at the time, this class represented a watershed generation — an important transitional time in American history. We grew up in the serenity of the 1950s, with a grandfather figure in the White House. We enjoyed a stable economy and could purchase a gallon of gas for thirty-four cents.

The world lived in peace, recovering from a recent world war, and the term "cold war" was a word our history teachers bantered about during discussions on current events. The world began to change in our senior year. At lunch, we used to engage in hot debates about the merits of electing Richard Nixon or John Kennedy. In the coming decade, the hopes fostered by the rhetoric of the young president disintegrated into the vivid realities of an Asian war, the delusion of assassinations, the divisive nature of the civil rights movement, the destructive nature of drugs and a discordant counterculture.

We may have graduated in 1961 as naive urchins in the big, bad world, I thought, *but most of us learned how to develop a callous demeanor about events that ripped apart the tapestry of our nation. I wonder how the lives of my classmates were affected by their first decade after graduation. I'm sure I'll hear more stories from people who actively tried to find answers and those who hunkered down and found sanctuary in Oak Ridge.*

I looked up from the packet and noticed the stands filling with students, parents and more alumni. The football teams warming up on the field looked like two small armies preparing to do battle. I opened my corduroy jacket and leaned back to soak in the warm September sun — a brilliant autumn day. I recalled another time when I sat in the stands watching a game, surrounded by friends, plotting how to score a case of beer to take to the gravel pit after the sock hop. *Those were the simple days with no worries, no car payment and no mortgage payment,* I thought.

The arrival of a boisterous woman with bleached-blonde hair interrupted my reflections. She wore a large-brimmed, orange hat and carried a *Go Huskies* sign in one hand. She had trouble negotiating the cement stairs and tried to steady her ascent by using people on the end of each row as her personal crutch. Her loud voice and body movements indicated she had been drinking before the game — probably at some private alumni party.

I shook my head and studied her movements with greater interest. Finally, I realized I knew her: Joy Sedgwick, my old drinking buddy. She's the woman who vowed to go to college and earn her M.R.S. degree. I now had a reason to move down into the section reserved for the alumni and chat with her.

I slid into the seat next to Joy and watched her body sway to the beat of the high school pep band. "Hello, Joy, interested in a forest preserves woodsy tonight? I'll bring the beer." Her arms looked like a kaleidoscope of flashing gems adorned with massive diamond bracelets and a huge rock on each finger. She waved her hands about with gestures that flaunted her excessive wealth.

Hearing my offer, the woman abruptly turned to look at me. Then, she gave me a huge bear hug and shouted, "Mark Pierce, you old dog. Of course, I'd go on a woodsy with you anytime. In fact, I think I did every time you asked."

"You sure did, Joy, … and we did a little skinny dipping in the pond as well."

"You still remember that stuff?"

"Not until this very minute. It was our secret back then," I responded.

"Yeah, you and the entire track team knew about it, didn't they?"

I grinned, "I think the word got out, but they didn't hear it from me."

"Well, I'm an old gal now and don't want to get naked in public. But some parts of this body are a lot younger than others, if you get my drift," she said jabbing me in the ribs. Her suggestive stage whisper made several people sitting nearby giggle. Joy placed both hands under her large breasts and continued, "For example, these are new ... got 'em last year, right after my fourth divorce. How do you like 'em? Wanna feel?"

"Very nice, I think, but I'll pass on the *Charmin* test." I felt embarrassed drawing unwanted attention to us. I craved anonymity, but Joy's loud, bellowing voice countered my desire.

Trying to change the subject, I asked, "Joy, I take it you got your M.R.S. degree?"

"Hell, Mark," she slurred, "you mean, Marrying Rich Studs? I've got four of those degrees hanging on my garage wall, nailed up right next to my scrotum trophies. In fact, I got one hanging in each of my four garages."

"So, you'd call your *educational pursuit* a success," I teased.

"Success? Not only was I a success, but the divorces alone put me on easy street."

"Do you intend to get married again?" I asked.

"Hell, no. I don't have any use for another penis waving around my bedroom. If I ever showed interest in another man, he'd have to own a bank account the size of Texas." The crowd around us burst into laughter again. She finished the sentence and removed a silver, diamond-inlaid flask from her purse and took a long drink.

Handing it to me, she asked, "Want a swig?"

"No, thanks." I looked over my shoulder and said, "Joy, I have to leave and meet a friend. It's been nice seeing you again. It looks as if life in Texas has been very good for you."

"See ya', Markie."

I negotiated the steps to return to my secluded place in the stands and heard Joy's voice bellow to the crowd around her, "Did you know Markie and I used to get drunk and go shh…inny sipping together? Did I ever tell you about the cute little freckle on the end of his …." She stumbled to find the right word to use in public, as if it mattered, and said, … "his thingy?" Onlookers laughed, and I disappeared into the throng of people now filling the bleachers.

Money and marriage does not guarantee happiness, I thought. *I got married for all the wrong reasons.*

I met Vicki on one of my jobs. More motivated by my groin than my heart, marriage sounded like something fun to try. At the age of twenty-six, I became a father. I had no clue about raising kids, but a second one appeared shortly after the first. Born two years apart, the children became inseparable friends. Their eyes had such intensity, curiosity and enthusiasm for life. The divorce five years later changed all that. When their mother moved out of state, she took the boys with her. My emotional relationship with my sons became distant and cold; I now see them once or twice a year. They refer to me as their sperm donor. I grimaced. *I even failed at being a father.*

A voice interrupted my thoughts as I climbed into the obscurity of the top bleachers. "Mark Pierce, it *is* you. How are you doing?"

I turned and looked into the face of my old elementary school chum, Robert Hastings. He stood in the aisle with an outstretched hand. A much younger woman hung on his arm.

"Robert, you look great. When you enlisted in the Marines, I thought I'd never see you again — especially when Vietnam got rolling."

"Remember, I was a tough dude, ... and could always whip you. I knew how to take care of myself, and even had two tours of duty in Nam. I had a good head for logistics, and they turned me into a quartermaster. ... Never picked up a gun except to hand it to someone."

"What have you been doing since?" I asked. Robert had been my nearest neighbor, and we spent a lot of time playing together — from toy soldiers to board games. When we entered high school, personal interests sent us in different directions. Robert dedicated his life to a church youth group and Junior ROTC. On the other hand, I roamed the streets for entertainment.

"Once I got out of the service," he continued, "I came back to Oak Ridge and joined the police force. Had an opportunity for early retirement and took it. Now I live in Grand Junction, Colorado."

"Good for you," I added, turning my attention to the lovely woman holding onto Robert's arm. I spotted a wedding ring and asked, "Are you going to introduce me to your beautiful bride?"

"This is Marilyn. Literally, she is my gift from God."

"Robert, I didn't know God delivered gifts like her."

"No, no, you don't understand. Marilyn came to me because of my connection to God."

I studied the serious look on Robert's face and then shifted my focus to Marilyn. She nodded her head in agreement. They had a story to share, and their body language begged me to listen.

"The game won't start for a while. Tell me how God sent Marilyn to you."

The three of us sat down, and Robert began his tale.

"If you remember, my parents got divorced just after I turned twelve. Jackie Sabaro, the woman who lived down the block from our house, took me under her wing."

"I remember her — that young newlywed who moved in several doors down from me — the good-looking lady with long, dark-black hair. I recall she got really involved with her church, right?"

"Yeah, that's the one. She felt sorry for me and started taking me to her church. I really liked it. Initially, I just wanted to be with her, but after a while I made friends with kids in the youth group."

"You're telling me a twelve-year-old kid fell in love with a beautiful woman in her early twenties."

"Yup. It impressed me that an older woman, close to my age, would care enough about a scrawny, pimple-faced kid who was emotionally lost. She became my guardian angel."

I glanced at Marilyn as she tightened her grasp on Robert's arm and smiled. *Such a patient, supportive woman,* I thought.

Robert continued, "Then when I turned fifteen, Jackie got pregnant and her husband got transferred to Texas, and they moved away. The loss devastated me – a personal disaster for a moonstruck kid. I tried to stay connected to the church, but it just wasn't the same without Jackie."

"I don't remember you as a church boy in our senior year. In fact, by that time you were one of the regulars who played 'quarry quest' with us."

Robert patted Marilyn's arm and looked at me. "I regret those crazy days, Mark. That's what did you in, wasn't it?"

I ignored his reference and pushed to hear the rest of his tale. "How does Marilyn fit in?"

"That's where God entered my life again — almost unbelievable. Jackie sent me a letter from Texas telling me she had the baby. A year later, she and her husband took another job in California and moved again. That's when I lost track of her completely."

I couldn't tell if they were ignoring my question or having fun stretching out the story. Marilyn noticed the confused look on my face and placed a hand on my arm. "All of this will make sense in a minute. Robert loves telling all the details, and I can't hear it enough. It's wonderful to be so blessed."

Robert continued, "Twenty years later, I worked for the Oak Ridge police force. An officer got sick one day, and I agreed to take a double shift and cover his duty assignment. I had to manage traffic control for a funeral."

"You see," Marilyn broke in, "my grandmother lived in Oak Ridge and passed away. I came back with Dad to attend the funeral. When I was standing outside to get some fresh air, this patrol officer hit on me." She smiled and looked at Robert. "We clicked right away, exchanged e-mail addresses and started corresponding. Eventually, I invited him to visit me in Grand Junction to meet my family."

"I used my vacation time to go see Marilyn," Robert added. "When I rang the bell, Marilyn's mother opened the door. Immediately, the woman threw her arms around me and said, 'God has brought you back to us.' "

"I was stunned," Robert said.

Marilyn clarified the details so I could understand the significance of the moment as well. "You see, my mother's name is Jackie, Jackie Sabaro, the same woman who knew Robert when he was twelve."

"Are you serious? What a coincidence."

"No coincidence. God connected my mother and Robert through the church, and they were meant to find each other, again. Neither Mother nor Robert knew he had fallen in love with me, Jackie's daughter — the child born in Texas when Robert was fifteen. He didn't know it was me because Mom and Dad got divorced and she remarried. My stepfather adopted me, and I took his last name."

Marilyn and Robert exchanged a kiss and a lingering hug. I watched the two embrace and smiled at their good fortune.

"When I returned to Oak Ridge, I discovered the force had negotiated a great early retirement package for us long-term officers. I thought God provided me with another sign. He opened a new direction for me, so I left Oak Ridge and moved to Grand Junction to be with Marilyn and Jackie."

"We were married almost thirty years ago," Marilyn added.

"And the age difference was never a factor?"

"In God's eyes, time is meaningless. God wanted us to be husband and wife."

"That's an amazing story," I said.

The PA system interrupted our conversation and announced the beginning of the game. Robert and Marilyn shook my hand, excused themselves and found their seats. I watched them cuddle and smiled. *How could the presence of God motivate Robert to leave Oak Ridge and find a woman he once met by accident?* I thought. *But, had it really been an accident? Who knows? What did Father McCray say? ... God moves in mysterious ways.*

"And you'll always love me won't you?"
"Yes."
"And the rain won't make any difference?"
"No."
— Ernest Hemingway

Chapter Eighteen:
Half-Time Highlights

"To keep our faces toward change
and behave like free spirits in the
presence of fate is strength undefeatable."
— Helen Keller

The crowd settled in and watched the first half of a typical high school football game. Both teams moved the ball up and down the field. Several fumbles interrupted the action; a couple of bad penalty calls followed, then a half-dozen short punts and a touchdown or two completed the action. The skill-level of football players at Oak Ridge had not improved much since my era — or, more likely, that's the realistic nature of high school football.

At halftime, the high school band marched onto the field and played through well-rehearsed formations. In the middle of their program, the young musicians created a square that encircled a group of old-timers, former band members from our class, playing their own set of songs. The tunes sounded pretty good, coming from rusty, old horn and drum players. The two bands played the school's fight song, followed by the crowning of the current homecoming king and queen by the 1961 royal court. I spotted a smiling Julie Simms and Tad Summerfield, a popular couple back in my day and the '61 homecoming king and queen. They enthusiastically waved to an appreciative crowd. *Nice touch*, I thought, and I made my way to the bathroom before the second half started.

I emerged from the restroom and headed for the concession stand just as the band left the field. I stared at the limited, bland menu. *Too bad I can't get a beer and a hot dog,* I thought. *But, that's the kind of thing that would upset the school board ... even though we're celebrating our fiftieth. No matter, I'll soon have a beer at Red's Lounge when I meet with Carol.*

I bought my second hot dog and soft drink and headed for the bleachers. On my way, I spotted Donna Douglas walking ahead of me. She and I frequently occupied adjacent chairs in the principal's conference room. Like me, she played the system and was frequently sent out of class for violating some classroom rule. In high school, Donna displayed a hot temper and sarcastic, biting tongue. Those endearing qualities put her at a great disadvantage when dealing with no-nonsense instructors. Like me, Donna liked to challenge the frail egos of teachers who struggled to teach uninspired youth the essentials of their subject matter. Our response to these shortcomings forged an unlikely friendship and provided a meeting place for us to compare notes.

Mr. Beyer, the school principal, put every wayward child through the same drill. Armed with pen and paper, he asked us to explain, in detail, the reason for our being sent out of class to his office. Our convoluted sentences, combined with spelling and grammar errors, must have been fairly amusing to the patient man. But, this ritual gave us time to express our anger in writing and to let our adolescent emotions dissipate. Thus restrained, we could deal with the inevitable consequences of our errant behavior. For an old school principal, he proved to be a good child psychologist.

"Hey, sweetheart, writing any excuses for the man lately?" I shouted.

She turned around and instantly recognized me. "How's my favorite detention partner?" she asked, slugging me on the shoulder. *What's with women,* I pondered, *does a man's arm provide an easy target for pent-up, female aggression?*

"Still showing off your left hook," I said, rubbing my arm in faux pain.

"That's the only way I ever got people to respect me," she responded. "How you doing, mister?"

"Can't complain," I said.

"I've heard different."

"I'll bet you have, but let's not go there." I studied her adult features and smiled, "So, you finally graduated from detention. What did you do after high school?"

"Very funny, Mark," she answered with a smile. "Actually, I turned out to be an intelligent person. I discovered most of my abhorrent behaviors came from being bored."

"What do you mean?" I asked.

"After graduation, I decided to get as far away as I could. President Kennedy's altruism, you know, … *ask not what your country can do for you, but what you can do for your country.* Sounds corny now, but back then it struck a chord and motivated me to do something. I wanted an adventure in my life. Back then, women weren't supposed to be strong and independent, but I wanted to prove them wrong."

"Let me guess. You joined the Peace Corps."

"You bet. After a few months of training, I spent my first assignment in Barbados — two great years."

"What do you mean your first assignment?"

"It worked out well and people appreciated everything I did. In spite of my gender, I felt needed and had the skills to instill hope in people. After Barbados, I volunteered for another two years in Senegal, and then spent time in Malaysia."

"I'm impressed. Never figured you for one of those volunteer liberal types."

"It took me a while to mature and figure out what I wanted to do with my life. At age twenty-four, I returned to the states and began helping people in my own country."

"The late sixties had to be a tough time for volunteer work."

"Yeah. I returned and didn't recognize the place. People split over the war, social upheaval, and the counter culture."

"After being gone for almost a decade, you must have felt like a stranger."

"With all the chaos taking place, I couldn't settle down to do anything and felt restless, like the rest of the nation."

"What did you do?"

"I paid my dad four hundred dollars for his old Plymouth Valiant and hit the road. I wanted to find peace somewhere, anywhere. First, I headed to the east coast, ran through the south and then west."

"How did you pay for things?"

"I worked as a waitress, hotel night clerk and then took odd jobs as they came my way."

"Sounds fascinating."

"Yeah, but I struggled through all of it. I wanted to discover why the American life I once knew had fallen apart. I felt disconnected and uncomfortable everywhere I went."

"When did you find the answer?"

"By the fall of 1975, I ended up in Flagstaff, Arizona, and enrolled at Northern Arizona University. My parents supported my choice to settle down and get a college degree by paying the tuition. Imagine that, a thirty-plus-year-old freshman."

"Did the *ancient* student make it through college?"

"I spent five years at NAU and graduated with a double major. Pretty damn good, I'd say."

"Don't tell me ... let me guess. You majored in sales. With all of those tunnel passes you sold to freshmen in high school, I'd think you'd be a natural."

"Is that the most significant thing you remember about me?" she laughed.

"Donna, you became the tunnel pass legend at Oak Ridge — that is, until they discovered your scam and made you serve time in detention."

Donna smiled broadly and reflected, "Yeah, those were good times. I made about two hundred dollars every September until that pimple-faced little nerd, Betsy Singer, ran to the principal and *"ratted* me out."

I grinned at the memory. An underground tunnel connected our main campus building with the field house. It ran under a practice field and protected students from inclement weather. Donna, as *Queen of the Tunnel*, positioned herself at its entrance and extracted money from small female students by her physical intimidation alone. Crowds of upper classmen often gathered to watch her work. However, it took the naiveté of a tiny girl, the daughter of a school board member, to break up her lucrative racket.

"In college, I had a double major: public relations and marketing."

"What did you end up doing after college?"

"I searched the Internet for best places to live and then headed for Portland, Oregon. No job, no friends, no apartment — just lived on my confidence to get a good job —something that would satisfy my need for adventure."

"That's where your streak of independence helped, I bet. Did the move work out for you?"

"Within two weeks, I had rented a condo and landed a job as a project manager with a construction company — not just a construction company, but *the* primo construction company in the city. They built most of the office buildings in town."

"Very impressive," I commented.

Donna acknowledged my compliment and continued, "It helped that I was a mature, intelligent, worldly woman and not an inexperienced college graduate. Within a year, this novice, female project manager became the head honcho in charge of a major construction site. I spent most of my time barking orders at a bunch of old construction salts who had been on the job for almost thirty years. They respected my work because I knew my stuff."

"How long did you stay with the company?"

"Within five years, my restlessness kicked in again, and I had to do something else. So, I moved to Guatemala and worked in the company's international division."

"Amazing."

"All my life, that restless behavior has been a blessing and a curse. I'd work with a company for a few years and then take a sabbatical leave to get back to my need to volunteer."

"You're both a rolling stone and a bleeding heart liberal," I teased.

"Something like that," she countered. "The remainder of my career has been one adventure after another. I'm quite pleased."

"I'm happy for you, Donna. Obviously, you had too much energy to live in the confines of Oak Ridge. I'm glad you had the courage to follow your heart. You earned the credentials and had the moxie to succeed. You must have been an inspiration to other women who followed your example."

"Thank you, Mark. That means a lot coming from you. In my old age, I've slowed down a bit, but travel a lot. I've moved to Florida. It's warm, and I am close to cruise lines and convenient flights to Europe."

"Any time for romance?"

"No time for a relationship. Most people can't keep up with me."

I laughed and told her she needed to go hunting for someone like herself.

The crowd erupted, signaling the beginning of the second half. I gave Donna a quick hug and told her I'd see her at the party, but I knew I wouldn't. She made me feel guilty. To see what she did to turn her life around and to find her place made me bristle with jealousy. She and I went down similar paths, and she made it work. I didn't. I kicked a plastic cup lying on the cement in front of me and cursed my fate. "Stop it, Mark, self-loathing will not get you through this afternoon." I spoke to the cup and crushed it underfoot.

"Now is no time to think
of what you do not have.
Think of what you can do with that there is."
— Ernest Hemingway

Chapter Nineteen:
The Art of Dancing With Life

"In order to succeed, people need a sense of self-efficacy, struggle together with resilience to meet the inevitable obstacles and inequities of life."
— Albert Bandura

I made my way up the stadium stairs and caught a glimpse of Mary's three thugs scanning the stands. I quickly ducked below the heads of people already seated and found an empty place to hide. I craned my neck to see if the move worked. My unexpected fright distracted me, and I barely felt the gentle tap on the shoulder. A voice said, "Mark Pierce, ... I thought it was you."

Startled by his touch, I jumped, turned toward the intruder and gazed into the soft eyes of Art Gentry. "Art, how are you doing?"

"I'm getting by," he responded and sat down on the step next to me.

"When people tell me their 'getting by,' it usually means things could be better. What's going on, Art?"

I paused long enough to take a good look at my former classmate. Like most of us, he showed signs of thinning hair and graying around the temples. However, I noticed a distant, pained look on his face. I put my arm around him and offered a brief hug.

Throughout high school, Art sat next to me in homeroom, that artificial period providing the school administration time to communicate with students. We tuned out the drone voice of Mr. Beyer as he read the daily announcements and missed most of the essential news of the day. Art and I spent time sharing opinions about school life, good-looking girls, politics and teachers. Fifty years later, here we sat, huddled together on the steps of the football stadium, engaged in another homeroom chat.

"You took off in a hurry after your catastrophe and never said goodbye to your old pals. What gives?"

"Yeah, I know," ignoring his comment. "Not important, but I'm more curious about you." I continued, "What happened to you after graduation?"

I watched Art's eyes light up, and he enthusiastically shared his experience. "After high school, I got a job at an electrical parts warehouse on the north side located near skid row. For a lad of eighteen, this was quite an eye opener, to see life at its lowest — human beings scratching out a living from day-to-day, largely living off a little food and a lot of cheap alcohol."

"Wow, that must have been a huge learning experience for a suburban white kid."

"Yeah, every day I saw things that surprised me. Growing up in Oak Ridge sheltered us from a lot. On the way to work, I had to walk five blocks through retched humanity and witness sights and sounds that not many people ever see. I looked at one man lying in a doorway at 6 a.m., in minus fifteen degree temps using bottles of alcohol as personal anti-freeze. Lucky he didn't die trying to stay warm. Another guy sat by a fire plucking the feathers off dead pigeons and cooking them to sell. He'd take the money, buy booze and be drunk by the time I got off work."

"See, Art," I said, "I always suspected that Rock Cornish game hens were actually processed Chicago pigeons. You've never seen them photographed together, have you?"

He smiled and went on.

"After two years at a dead-end job and my daily exposure to the street people, I learned I had to make something of myself. The kind of things I witnessed scared me. To me, the difference between success and failure in life was to maintain a positive attitude. If I gave up and rolled over, I could become like the men I passed in the streets every day."

"I enrolled in a technical school and studied science and in three years obtained an Associate's Degree in Applied Science. In school, I met the love of my life and married her. That, friend, added a treasure to my world. I wasn't alone anymore, and she became a partner to share the struggles and triumphs."

"You're saying your wife gave you stability and the courage to take risks."

"Right, we got out of here, and my first job landed us in Long Island, New York, where I worked at Brookhaven National Laboratory. I became a main control room operator of the 33 billion electron-volt accelerator. During the early and mid-60s, scientists started exploring the nucleus of the atom and its composition. They conducted experiments on the machine. I became a key part of that cutting edge research.

"How did being away from Oak Ridge change you?"

"When you leave your family to start a new life, you're lucky if you're married. My wife and I bonded. We learned to depend on just ourselves, and our shared experiences formed a deep love and respect for each other. I think being away from our folks may have been the best thing for the longevity of our marriage."

"I'm impressed with your personal loyalty and commitment."

"The time away from home taught me a sense of self-confidence. I thought I could do anything. The job lasted three and a half years, and then we came back to Oak Ridge so I could get more training. I got a job at the Fermi Laboratory in Batavia, similar to the one in New York, but I ran the main control room of a twelve billion electron accelerator and managed projects created by local university scientists."

Art paused and smiled about that accomplishment and then continued.

"I worked at the lab for three years, but the commute took its toll on me. So, I resigned, and Zenith Radio hired me as a technician supervisor, and spent ten years with them — turned out to be the best and happiest years on a job. Our research staff consisted of approximately two hundred and fifty of the brightest minds in the industry. For ten years, we experimented with developing a flat-panel television, using the limited knowledge of that time. Our group worked on developing a thin film transistor; while other teams worked on the phosphates for the screen and plasma tubes. Looking back at our task, our ideas outpaced technology."

"Did you stay with Zenith?"

"No, I got a job at Tektronix in Oregon, which makes excellent electronics measurement equipment. That job lasted five years, and then I got laid off again."

"Seems to have been an unexpected pattern in your life."

"Yeah, and by the age of fifty-five, I was determined not to work for someone else again."

"You took another risk?"

"After searching for the right business venture, my wife and I started a rubber stamp company. We named it Liberty Rubber Stamp, after the Statue of Liberty and Ellis Island, where my parents arrived in 1922. If it wasn't for my mother's passion to come to the United States and have a better life, I probably wouldn't be here today."

"Those parental values play a big part in shaping your life, don't they?"

"Absolutely. We operated the stamp company as a home-based business and, ten years later, sold it for a nice profit and retired. Doing your own thing ... that's the most important lesson I learned. When you work for someone else, you risk compromising much of your passion."

"I'm impressed with your story ... from the streets of Chicago to owning your own business in Oregon."

"Oh, my friend, life gives you many lessons to learn. It often plays tricks on a person's ego. You think you've got it made, and then God throws you a curve ball."

"Did you hit it anyway?"

"Hit it? Hell, I almost struck out. In 1994, physicians said I suffered from congestive heart failure, and the condition deteriorated over time. I had no energy to run the business, let alone follow a daily routine. They tried surgery, but it failed. My heart's ejection fraction is too low."

"I have no clue what that means?"

"It ain't rocket science, but the ejection fraction is the number that tells physicians how much blood pumps into the body with each heartbeat. A healthy heart pumps about sixty percent of the blood coming into the left ventricle. With me, the old ticker now operates at twenty percent."

"Sounds bad, Art."

"Yeah, it's a bummer. I get tired quickly, but the heart is a muscle, so I do cardio exercises and lift weights to keep my body working as healthy as it can be."

"Is there hope for another operation or something?"

"Yeah, they can inject my heart with my stem cells. In theory, it should repair the heart, but I have to lose weight first. It's really hard when you get to my age, but I am determined to do it."

"How do you spend your time waiting?"

"I use the secret practiced by my old homeless friends back in Chicago. I personally call it *Art's rules of tenacity and resilience.*"

"Art's rules?"

"Some people label my condition a death notice, but not me. After I retired, I refused to quit. With the money we saved through investments, I decided to *play* every day I have left to live ... or, until the operation improves my health."

"How do you play, Art?"

"I have a passion for the sea and delight in booking cruises every chance I get. I especially enjoy those re-positioning cruises that take ships from a summer port to a winter destination, and back again."

"That's a marvelous way to spend your time."

"It sure is. Where else can you get waited on hand and foot, have maid service clean your room, eat any time you feel hungry, enjoy live entertainment and sail into a different port every day or so?"

"It must be a blast."

"Yes, I find killer deals on the Internet and ask friends to join me. I get better rates if I can book a block of cabins. Every trip turns into an ongoing party. When I get tired and can't keep up with the younger crowd, I excuse myself and take a nap."

"I'd say you're living life with intensity. You clearly know what to do with the time you have remaining in your life."

"Here's how I see it. We are all travelers in time and observers of life. Life is a world of duality — positive and negative aspects — everywhere and everything. I observe other players to see which direction they choose. Choice has its good and bad aspects. Some people become paralyzed when negative things happen, and others make the most of it. For me, I stay on the positive path — observe, participate and play. That's the secret of happiness."

"I really admire your courage and ability to take control of your life." I looked at Art and thought, *It's embarrassing to compare my life to anything Art has accomplished.* Then, I watched Art's body begin to sag.

"I need to go back to the hotel and take a quick nap. I want to be able to kick up my heels at the celebration tonight."

I gave Art a warm hug. "Thanks for sharing your story. I needed to hear that message. Your insights will get me through a troublesome appointment I have later this afternoon."

"Glad I could help. Just remember, none of us know how much time we have in life, but it's important to pay attention and find joy in every opportunity."

"Thanks. I'll try to remember that from now on."

Art carefully negotiated each stair, making his way down, out of the bleachers. *That quiet kid in homeroom*, I mused, *could have been the life coach I wish I had known back then. Today he loosely carries Machu Picchu in his back pocket, even though it could fall out at any moment, but at least he's found it.*

"Courage is grace under pressure."
— Ernest Hemingway

Chapter Twenty: Confronting the Past

"Apology is a lovely perfume; it can transform the clumsiest moment into a gracious gift."
— Margaret Lee Runbeck

I left the game and headed for Red's Lounge. Fear of being accosted by oversized goons forced me to glance over my shoulder as I walked, but nobody followed me. I planned to be at the bar before Carol arrived, so I could rehearse my words. I found Red's and walked into a dimly lit room. My eyes adjusted, and I located a small booth across from the bar.

An alert waitress appeared to take my order, and I informed her of Carol's expected arrival. Carol came through the door just before 4 p.m. I rose and gave her a hug. To my surprise and delight, she remained entwined in my arms for a long moment. I barely moved and looked at her. She had aged softly. Her light brown hair, probably colored now, smelled like lilacs. Carol's eyes still had the same mischievous twinkle I remember from high school. *She was always such a flirt*, I smiled at the thought. Following an old pattern from fifty years earlier, I softly kissed her forehead. To my surprise, she didn't pull away. Her arms encircled my body again, and we lingered in a warm embrace.

She finally stepped back and smiled. Her face revealed no sign of the pent-up anger I heard when we talked on the phone. The meeting of two former high school lovers provided a mixture of joy and sadness. Tears filled our eyes, and we hugged again. We embraced in the kind of moment you rarely experience in a lifetime, nothing planned — spontaneity ruled and encircled us like a warm blanket. Finally, we exhaled, swiped at our tears and sat in the booth across from each other.

I extended my hands across the table and, like the past, she placed hers in mine. Our fingers entwined — the moment seemed natural and comforting. It ended when our waitress returned to take Carol's order.

"I don't mean to interrupt, but I wanted to bring your beer before it gets warm." Looking at Carol, she asked, "Can I get something for you, honey?"

"Yes, I'll have a glass of Pinot Grigio, please."

The waitress brought her a glass of wine, and Carol took a sip. With the spell of our initial encounter broken, her expression grew serious. A flood of unexpressed questions that linger in the recesses of her mind needed to be released. She pulled her hand back and stared into my eyes. A cool, businesslike expression replaced her initial gentleness.

"Even after all these years, Mark, I still deserve an explanation."

"I agree. What do you want to know?"

"Why did you leave without saying goodbye? You crushed my heart." She hesitated long enough to take a deep breath to keep from crying. She seemed determined to remain strong. Her eyes refocused on me, and her jaw tightened.

"I left because I was confused, scared and didn't know how to deal with the truth. I felt ashamed and thought it would be better to leave. If they all hated me, … well, let them."

Carol looked into my eyes and said nothing. She slowly ran her hand across her forehead and then became distracted by turning the stem of the wine glass in front of her.

This conversation will be more challenging than I anticipated, I thought. I exhaled and began to explain. "After *that* night, I couldn't eat or sleep. My parents isolated me from everyone — no phone calls, no visitors. Worst of all, the concussion blurred my memory. I couldn't remember the details of the accident. I recall slamming on the brakes and then … nothing."

Carol sat quietly studying the wine glass and occasionally glancing at me as I revealed each thought. She fidgeted and seemed distant.

I touched the scars on my head and grimaced, remembering the pain when I awoke in the hospital. "The head wounds kept me bedridden. My throat injury prevented me from speaking above a whisper. With graduation a week away, everything became a blur."

"I remember, Mark. I wanted to see you, but your parents refused to let me in the house. They blamed me for what happened to you," she said. "But, you always knew I'd be there for you, didn't you? If only you had called, I'd have come right over."

"I know, but I felt so guilty for what I did to mess up so many lives. My parents and school counselor agreed to send my school work and final exams home. They kept me isolated until the graduation ceremony. The principal didn't want me to march at graduation, but my parents insisted. The compromise allowed me to walk across the stage to receive my diploma. I had to sit in a chair behind the curtains until the counselor read my name. It was humiliating, but I deserved it."

"Graduation was the first time I saw you since the night of the accident, and after that, I never saw you again, until today. Why did you leave so suddenly?" she begged.

"You heard them, Carol, when they read my name — remember the awkward silence, followed by the catcalls and boos. They hated me. I couldn't take it."

"So, you decided to run away — from us, from all of your pain? You took the coward's way out, Mark."

"Yes, I did. I couldn't face anybody." Then, looking into Carol's eyes, I added, "I didn't think I could even face you. So, I left without telling anyone."

"The thing that hurt the most was the illusion of our love. I thought it could withstand anything, but it had no depth, only empty words."

"I thought we were in love, too, but had no idea how to deal with the venom and hate that swirled around us. I thought they would turn on you because of our relationship. My god, even my parents couldn't deal with you. I left to try to feel normal again."

"Normal! How totally self-centered, Mark," she raised her voice. "No communication. No farewell. No *I love you*. I felt abandoned by the only person I had ever given my heart, soul and body to …." A steady stream of tears interrupted her tirade and formed tiny pools on the table.

I hung my head and sat quietly, giving her time to regroup. I deserved all of her wrath. To my surprise, she stopped, sniffed and wiped her eyes with a napkin. I looked at her and used my napkin to dry the tears that had fallen on the table.

"At this point, I can only say I'm sorry," I said. "I have no excuse for the scared, confused seventeen-year-old kid who had never faced that kind of thing before — or since, for that matter. After I left town, I fooled myself into thinking I'd come back or invite you to join me some day, but it didn't happen."

I paused and choked back my own tears. I felt nauseous, my heart pounding. I struggled to find the right words. "Life and circumstances … got in the way of love. I'm truly sorry for all the pain I caused — the actions of a stupid kid. I'm sorry … please … can you find it in your heart to forgive me?"

She ignored my apology and continued. "Mark, I loved you so much, and you deserted me. I felt so alone. But, after I got your postcard, my feelings changed. I felt used and thrown away. I was determined to block my memory of you, of us, forever, and move on."

"Did it work?"

"Yes, I went to college and discovered other men were attracted to me, not just a high school sweetheart. When I fell in love with one of them and he proposed, I married him."

"I'm glad you found yourself, Carol."

"To tell you the truth, Mark, Even then I was too young to get married. I realized I still loved you. I got married because I was afraid of being abandoned again. Eventually I learned to trust my husband, and Shawn never disappointed me. "

Her words pounded nails into my heart. I had run from my own pain, but now realized the greater distress I had brought Carol. Her comments made me feel small and fragile. She crushed my pathetic attempt to reconcile with her. I sat back in the booth and took a deep breath, saying nothing. Silence filled the space between us. I wanted to hide — to get back on the plane to San Francisco and discard this quest for redemption — to bury it where it had remained safely hidden for so long.

"Shawn and I lived together for forty-five great years," she continued. "Then last year, he suffered a stroke and died within a week."

"I'm sorry," I said, reaching out for her hand again.

Carol took my hands in hers and smiled. "You're just full of sorrow and apologies today, aren't you?" Her demeanor softened and suddenly her tension disappeared. I didn't understand her emotional shift. For the second time in the afternoon, she relaxed in my presence.

Sensing the change, I offered her a weak smile. "Yes, ma'am, I intend to be the most apologetic human being you have ever known."

"Well, you're certainly doing a good job of it. I'm sorry, myself, for dumping all that on you. I'm surprised those feelings have lingered inside me for so long."

"That's okay. I certainly deserve your wrath." I offered another weak smile.

She grinned, reached up and touched my hair. "Oh, what could have been," she mumbled. Then, her finger traced the faint series of scars on my forehead and the surgical mark left on my neck. "You got off lucky, Mark."

"Yes, I know. Did your tailbone ever heal?"

"No, you bastard," she snickered. "It only hurt when I gave birth. The four times I experienced the thrill of motherhood, I relished every opportunity to curse you." She laughed at the look of horror on my face and continued. "Now it only hurts when it rains." She looked into my eyes and said, "I guess I got off pretty easy, too."

"What happened to the other kids who got hurt that night?"

"Tim, you remember, survived without receiving a scratch. The guy has lived a charmed life."

"Tim," I shook my head, "always the lucky bastard in the group."

"Ironically, he believed that about himself as well and spent the rest of his career driving racecars for a living."

"That's the *Tim Saunders* I used to read about in the sports pages?"

"Yes. He retired a rich man at sixty, with a clean record — never in an accident or pileup."

"I can't believe his good fortune. And the rest?"

"Terry's arm mended, and he went on to college in the east somewhere — got married and moved to his wife's hometown in upstate New York. Beth cut her arm up pretty bad and had about forty stitches. After healing, she decorated her arm with a series of tattoos to blend in with the scars. It's a fascinating design and a great conversation starter. I saw it at the twenty-fifth reunion. After a couple glasses of wine, she's hilarious trying to explain the symbolic meaning of the tat. You might see her tonight."

"Oh, I'm overjoyed to hear that," I interjected. "I'll have a chance to apologize and then admire her personal artwork."

Carol laughed. "I always liked your irreverent sense of humor."

"Beth will be the easy apology," I said. "It sounds like she moved on to a normal, boring life as a mother and housewife."

"Yeah, but you'll have trouble apologizing to Ryan's brother and Ruth Ann's sister. You remember Ed and Theresa, don't you? They already know you've come back to town. You'll need to talk to them before you leave, … that is, if you're still serious about making amends for the past."

"Of course, I'm serious. But, I'm surprised Mary didn't organize more of the town vigilantes to hang me out at the quarry before I could infect the reunion."

"No," Carol snickered, "not the quarry … the rope might break, and you'd get away again."

"Very funny, lady," I laughed, "very funny."

"So, here's the deal," she said, growing serious again. "It took you a long time to give me your apology, but I know it came from your heart. … I accept it and forgive you."

I smiled at her, as my remaining tension slipped away.

"However," she continued in a somber tone, "that's because I walked away from it and lived to forgive you. Not everyone was that lucky. You can't go back and undo the damage you caused or apologize to ghosts. You've got to find a way to deal with the pain and memories that still linger with the survivors."

"I know, and I have only one day left to figure out how to do that. Have any ideas?"

"Ed and Theresa were freshmen when Ryan and Ruth Ann died. They never knew what *really* happened that night. You owe them an explanation. Perhaps, that will help."

"You're right," I said, letting my mind ponder her challenge.

"Tell you what I'll do, Mark. I'll give them a call and schedule a brunch at your hotel for tomorrow morning about 10 a.m. That should give you time to prepare."

"That'll work for me … but, I'm still at a loss to explain everything that went down. Some of the details never came back. Is there anything you can tell me about those last minutes that I may have blocked out?"

Carol said nothing, but I noticed her expression change, and she bit her lower lip. She refocused on the remains of the white liquid in her glass and downed the last sip. Her eyes moved to the napkin holder and then menu on the table in a successful attempt to avoid answering my question. Finally, she looked back at me and said, "No, Mark, I can't help you remember. I was as frightened as you were that night."

The waitress noticed our empty glasses and appeared at the table.

"Oh, my god, look at the time," Carol said. "I still have to shower and do my hair … got to run, Mark." She began to leave.

I got out of the booth and hugged her. "Thanks for being so generous with me," I said.

"You've got to remember I loved you … and probably still do. I would never choose to hurt you."

"Thank you," I whispered. "For the record, Carol, you need to know I always loved you."

"That's all I ever wanted to hear you say, Mark."

We parted, and I decided to walk the eight blocks back to my hotel. I took a deep breath and felt the cool, late afternoon air refresh me. Oak Ridge seemed like home again. Playfully, I swished through piles of leaves that had fallen on the sidewalk during the day, kicking at them like a nine-year-old. The intoxicating smell of fall rejuvenated me. I picked up my pace and sensed the ponderous weight of guilt lighten with each step. However, as I walked up the steps to my hotel, I hesitated and remembered Carol's words. *What did Carol mean when she said she would never choose to hurt me? How could she hurt me?*

"By then I knew that everything good and bad left an emptiness when it stopped. But if it was bad, the emptiness filled up by itself. If it was good you could only fill it by finding something better."

— Ernest Hemingway

Chapter Twenty-One: Inner Guidance

> "No man is great enough or wise enough for any of us to surrender our destiny to. The only way in which anyone can lead us is to restore to us the belief in our own guidance."
> — Henry Miller

Buoyed by a renewed sense of energy, I showered and dressed for the evening. I decided to walk the four miles to the Oak Ridge Country Club and forsake my usual cocktail at the hotel bar. After talking with Carol, I wanted to soak in the contentment I felt for the city again. I even looked forward to dealing with Mary's goons if I happened to run into them.

Looking at the place through adult eyes, I marveled at the architectural wonders crafted into many of the homes. I appreciated the huge, stately framed structures and their sweeping front porches. Houses in north Oak Ridge reflected a Victorian lifestyle that once graced this community. Many of the elegant homes along Pleasant Avenue could double as a setting for an antebellum Hollywood movie. They also reminded me of the town of Mayberry, and I expected to see Andy, Opie or Aunt Bee step out of the door with a glass of tea to share with this passing stranger.

My mind recalled the specter of social and political reality that lurked in the background of my high school years. Oak Ridge, primarily an all-white community, shared boundaries with cities that had greater racial diversity than our quaint village. Initially, class distinctions grew between people who lived in the affluent north Oak Ridge area and those less wealthy folks who lived south of the elevated tracks. The "L" ran parallel to Lake Street, and the street nearest the elevated tracks, South Avenue, marked the artificial boundary that divided the upper and middle class territory from those less financially solvent. Those who lived in south Oak Ridge stayed in apartments and smaller homes than the structures I now passed on my way to the country club.

The issue of race drew a bigger line than the delineation between the rich and poor. For years, Oak Ridge offered the last enclave for all-white residents near Chicago. The perception of black families moving to Oak Ridge posed a legitimate threat to the cultural uniformity of the city. Even before the civil rights movement reached its infancy, Oak Ridge experienced its own racial controversy. In 1950, Dr. James Parris purchased a home for his family in Oak Ridge. Before moving in, unknown parties bombed the house in an effort to discourage his decision to settle in the village. In spite of racial tensions in school, his son, James, Jr., graduated from Oak Ridge High School a couple of years before our class enrolled. We missed a lot of that tension, but inherited some of the subtle aftermath. James, Jr., graduated from college and eventually became a prominent lawyer in the civil rights movement. *Ironic,* I thought. *Today, sixty years later, Oak Ridge enjoys a national reputation for implementing a model diversity program.* The city officials even renamed my old elementary school after James' father — a symbolic tribute to his courage.

I got closer to the country club and experienced a deeper feeling of longing. *I ran away from this place due to a disaster of my own creation,* I thought. *In spite of everything that happened in-between, at this moment, I miss this place.*

Homesick? Sad? I didn't want to analyze it anymore. I walked into the country club and shook off the distraction.

The first person I spied at the reception table was Sally Broomfield — still in charge of matching people with name tags. Tonight, more comfortable than the first time we exchanged pleasantries, I approached her table and with a gallant gesture leaned across the table and gave her a quick kiss on the cheek.

"What was that for, Mark?" she blushed.

"Oh, just a thank you, Sally. You may not remember, but you were the first girl that ever kissed me … back in third grade, … and I wanted to return the favor."

She blushed again, touched her cheek, handed me a name tag and said, "Thank you, but I really don't remember."

Nice way to start the evening, I thought. *One of my fondest memories of the past meant nothing to her. Oh well, that was a very long time ago.*

I walked into the bar and requested a Rusty Nail. The man next to me concentrated on swishing his olive in a martini and finally looked at me. His stomach protruded over the belt like he had swallowed a beach ball. He sported a waxed handlebar mustache and wore dark-rimmed glasses. I got the impression he was a prosperous man, but I failed to recognize him and finally asked, "Excuse me, I'm Mark Pierce. I can't remember your name. I extended my hand.

"He grabbed my hand and vigorously shook it. "Mark Pierce. I thought I would never see you again. It's me, James Swinson."

"My god, life seems to have been quite good for you." I patted his stomach in jest. "You've put on several pounds. Did you eat that skinny 130-pound kid you used to be?"

"Hell, no. He was much too stringy for my taste."

"What are you doing now?" I asked.

"You must not go out to dinner much, do you?"

"No, it's not part of my lifestyle," I said.

"In the late 1970s, I graduated from the San Diego Culinary Arts school, got a scholarship to the Sorbonne in Paris and came back to open my first restaurant in Los Angeles."

"Very impressive," I said.

"Haven't you heard of the Saint James restaurant chain?" he continued with little modesty.

"That's you! It's difficult to believe a guy who loved beating up people for fun has become a restaurant entrepreneur. How did you make that transition? You were such a shit in high school."

"Nice, you remembered. You and I were always fighting in the Commons Park across from the school," he smiled. "And, we used to draw a big crowd, too."

"I sure do remember. If you and I got into it by 9 a.m., the whole school knew there'd be a show at three."

"Those were some good times, but after graduation all of that rough stuff carried over into my adult world. I was too dumb to go to school, so I got a job at a manufacturing plant in the suburbs. I ran with a fast crowd ... lots of booze, broads and drugs."

"What turned you into an oven jockey — sorry, a head chef and restaurateur?"

"Ted Foster."

"Who's that?"

"Someone who decided to save me. My life was going nowhere ... got nailed for several DUIs, and the judge sentenced me to take an alcohol/drug class. I thought it would be a waste of three Saturdays. My buddies sat in the back of the room, and I took a chair next to them, slumped down and tried to sleep through six hours of boring lecture."

"That sounds like you."

"Yeah, but this time it was different. I kept looking up at this Ted guy, and he always seemed to be watching me, talking directly to me."

"Did it creep you out ... as the kids say today?"

"Sort of, but a funny thing happened. I began listening to his words, and he started to make sense. Same thing happened during the next class and then the last one. When it ended, Ted asked me to join him for a cup of coffee — so, what the hell, I did."

"How did he turn your life around?"

"We just talked for hours about life, goals, passion, skills and attitude. ... Then he said, 'Based on what you have told me, James, I think you'd make a great restaurant owner and chef ... ever think about that?' " James ordered another martini, scrunched up his shoulders and admitted, "Ya know, Mark, I never had."

"Ted made a unique contribution to my life with his ability to encourage and support my thinking. He helped me become a waiter at a local restaurant to see if I liked the ambiance of the work. He helped me secure a student loan to go to culinary school. Then, Ted hooked me up with an anonymous donor who paid for a scholarship to study in Paris. I think Ted paid the bill, but he'll never admit it. When I returned, he lined up investors and helped me open my first restaurant."

"Why would he do all that for you?"

"I once asked him the same question, and do you know what he said?"

"What?"

"The man believed his purpose in life was to nurture the potential in others and help them achieve their dreams. Ted said some guy did it for him years ago, and he made a commitment to keep that gift cycle moving forward."

"He sounds like a closet philanthropist."

"I respect Ted as my mentor. I trust his vision, judgment and advice."

"So, you left the tough guy image in Oak Ridge and bought into the vision a mentor helped you define?"

"Yes, sir. I now own a chain of restaurants and make more money than I could have ever imagined. Had I stayed here, I'd be a nobody."

"You know, I once had that kind of mentor in my life."

"Really? Tell me about it."

"When I first started working for Standard Oil, I became Caleb's assistant. An old salt, Caleb had been in the field for almost forty years and developed a casual, almost intimate relationship with nature. He must have been sixty-two when I caught up with him in the Alaskan outback. Boy, did he resent playing nursemaid to a young greenhorn like me, and he let me know it at every opportunity. In time, however, he tolerated my presence because I showed him a desire to learn and, more importantly, paid attention to his wisdom."

"Your mentor wasn't anything like Ted."

"Not even close."

"Unlike my father, Caleb taught me about life through actions more than words. I watched the man engage in a love affair with nature — to listen, watch and sense the movement of animals, the wonder of change, and the cycles of growth and death. He'd constantly touch and smell plants and trees he passed on a trail. I learned how to respect the world and to see how it all fit together. Caleb never lectured me or shared his philosophy about life. He lived it."

"Nice memories, Mark."

"I know. The decade I worked with Caleb proved to be the most incredible experience I ever had. Unfortunately, it ended abruptly when the company 'retired' Caleb against his will. They didn't want an old man traipsing about in the wilderness on their expense account and costly insurance premiums. Even with all of Caleb's practical experience and wisdom, his career ended as a liability for the company and not an asset. I'll never understand corporate thinking. They throw away years of wisdom and experience when it's most needed. I wonder if that happened to other members of our class."

Before James could comment on my thought, a hostess stepped into the bar and announced dinner was being served. Dutifully, we finished our drinks and moved to the dining room to find our assigned tables.

"Perhaps as you went along
you did learn something.
I did not care what it was all about.
All I wanted to know was how to live in it.
Maybe if you found out how to live in it
you learned from that what it was all about."
— Ernest Hemingway

Chapter Twenty-Two:
A Little Rebellion Now and Then ...

"Human life is a continuous thread which each of us spins to his own pattern, rich and complex in meaning. There are no natural knots in it. Yet knots form, nearly always in adolescence."
— Edgar Z. Friedenberg

The reunion committee's exquisite planning impressed me. By a rough count, more than two hundred and fifty former classmates returned to the Oak Ridge celebration. Oak Ridge Country Club exceeded our expectations. The country club staff offered a sit-down dinner instead of standing in a traditional buffet line. Each of us had an assigned table, and a personalized place card identified our seats.

I found my spot and opened the decorative program sitting above my plate. A waiter brought pitchers of red and white wine to the table and poured a glass for me. The program listed the usual reunion activities and mock awards presented by our master of ceremonies, Frank Montain. The program also identified former classmates who had died over the years. *Well done*, I thought. Our dinner entree consisted of a choice between prime rib, chicken cordon bleu and a vegetarian selection. In addition to the main dish, the meal included salad, a twice-baked potato, a vegetable medley, chocolate mousse for dessert and, best of all for me, an abundance of wine to keep me relaxed. *The reunion committee went all out for this occasion,* I thought. *I'll send its members a thank you note after I get home.*

The program also announced that a three-piece string combo would be performing in an anteroom for those wanting to dance — a thoughtful touch for participants planning to stay in the dining room and talk with old friends. At our age, hearing often presents a challenge.

Looking at the name cards on either side of my seat, I wondered, *Who did the committee chose to seat next to me?* To my left, the card read, *Shirley Armstrong*, a name I didn't recognize. On the other side was *Bradley Rock*. Oh, god, — bad boy, Buddy Rock. *They decided to put the two troublemakers together*, I mused. Remembering a scene from *Alice's Restaurant*, I said aloud, "This must be the group W table."

In our day, Buddy became one of the school's hellions. When Buddy wasn't suspended, he spent more time in the principal's office than I did. Buddy, tough as a kid — even his name yelled "badass," broke the dress code every day by wearing blue jeans and a white T-shirt with a pack of cigarettes rolled-up under one sleeve. He became Oak Ridge's main "greaser" with hair slicked back. He looked like Fonzie on *Happy Days* ... long before the style became a *cool* fashion statement. Even though he looked like the Fonz, the difference ended there. Unlike Henry Winkler's character, *mean* became Buddy's preferred social style. He rode a fast motorcycle and scared the crap out of underclassmen. He had a lucrative scam going by extorting lunch money from small, pipsqueak freshmen boys who often peed in their pants when he approached. No, Buddy never resembled the affable Fonzie in attitude or persona.

An overweight, balding man interrupted my reminiscing with his awkward movement to sit down. I turned to him and said, "Buddy?"

"Mark Pierce, where the hell did they find you?"

"On an FBI most wanted bulletin," I said.

"Yeah, I saw your name just below mine," he retorted with a smile.

I couldn't believe it. The person sitting next to me was *the* Buddy Rock — a real sleazebag in high school, a mean SOB — now joking with me fifty years later. I remember that he not only broke all the rules at school, he also flattened me in a fight and busted my nose. Once we established a satisfactory pecking order, he decided to sell us all the beer and smokes we needed for parties at the quarry.

In our brief conversation, Buddy confessed he evolved from selling beer and marijuana into bigger gigs like cocaine sales and car theft. Right after he graduated high school, Buddy was arrested and spent some time at the Boys Reform School in St. Charles. When he turned eighteen, the judge gave him the choice to either join the army or spend the rest of his sentence in Joliet Prison. Not much of a choice — Uncle Sam gained a new recruit.

Buddy bragged that his stint in the army straightened him out. In fact, he signed up for another tour of duty, and this time requested Vietnam. By the end of the 1960s, Buddy became a hardened veteran and loved the army. The Oak Ridge bad boy found his calling and morphed into a Master Sergeant and trained new recruits at Fort Benning, Georgia. *Perfect,* I thought. *I can't believe Buddy got a job that paid him to pick on young kids — just like his days in high school.* He told me he retired from the army a couple of years ago and now performs volunteer services for a community where he lives in Arkansas.

How strange, I thought. *The renowned Oak Ridge bad boy had to leave parents, friends and school in order to learn self-discipline.* I'd been aware of the army's ability to turn rebellious youth into upright citizens, but I never would have guessed they could accomplish that miracle. Buddy turned to his right and began a conversation with the husband of another one of our classmates.

I looked up to see three linebackers watching me from across the room. I nonchalantly turned back to Buddy and put my arm around his shoulder. Buddy looked at me and smiled. The three amigos recognized that Buddy Rock and I had been reacquainted as friends, and they walked away. I thought, *It's not what you know, but who you know that makes a difference. Old cliché, but it works.*

I now focused on the slender woman who slipped into her seat next to me. I glanced at a fit, attractive lady sipping her chardonnay and looking around the room. I didn't recognize her.

"Hi, my name is Mark Pierce." I offered her a hand and then dropped it immediately. "I know you ..., but you're not Shirley Armstrong."

"You should know me, Mark. You, Buddy and I spent a lot of time in detention together."

That comment caught Buddy's attention, and he quickly looked over at her. "If it isn't shitty Shirley Schultz," he shouted. He laughed and nodded hello in her direction.

"Right at you, big guy. Did you actually pay for your meal ticket tonight, or did you lean on some little guy outside the country club?"

"Ah, Shirley," he countered, "just as sweet as ever. Nice to see you again, babe."

"Still haven't lost that old sexist touch, have you, Buddy?" she countered. "What happened? Were you locked up in some jail cell and missed the gender equality movement?"

"Very funny, Shirl ...," he started to retort, and I interrupted.

"Now, kids, stop your bickering. You just reminded me of too many vivid memories of the old days ... and most of those I want to forget."

The three of us smiled like it happened yesterday. The conversation would have continued, but Buddy jumped up to greet one of his former gang members, and now I claimed Shirley's attention for myself.

"How did you become Shirley Armstrong? Get married or something?"

"Nope, never got married ... just changed my name to lose the *shitty Shirley Schultz* moniker. I've been too busy to think about getting married."

"Busy doing what?" I pursued.

"You can't call me a rolling stone, but I sure moved a lot of black dirt in my day. I caused a lot of trouble in high school and realized I'd never be satisfied with anything that most people considered normal. After high school, I traveled a bit. My parents gave me a car and suggested I go visit my aunt in Missouri — liked it there so much I decided to stay all summer. Aunt Gracie had a huge garden and a thing for plants. She talked to them as if each row of veggies had a personality — like they were people. After tending, nurturing and finally harvesting vegetables, I got hooked."

"How did that change your life?"

"My physician told me about the mood altering effects of light deprivation. That explanation turned out to be the reason why I became shitty Shirley in the first place. I acted out in high school because of the long Illinois winters. The summer farming experience at Aunt Gracie's encouraged me to look for an outside job. I enrolled at Cal Poly in San Luis Obispo, California, where I earned a degree in agricultural sciences. Stayed out there and got a job with the Pacific Northwest Seed Growers Association in Washington State in 1966."

"How long did that last?"

"About fifteen years. I was a state ag-agent and spent most of my time with the farmers and ranchers around the state. They trusted me. Old guys took this young girl under their wing and taught me the practical stuff you learn in the fields."

"You made a transition from Oak Ridge to the great outdoors by shedding all the trappings of city life," I said.

"Yup. I started eating right and lost all that excess weight I put on as a kid. Worked in the fields every day and got fit. I became a new person and decided to change my name as well. Shirley Armstrong — you know like our childhood hero, Jack Armstrong."

"Oh, now I get it."

"The best part of the transition was getting paid to be outside and to participate with others who loved the land like I did. Every year these old farmers gathered in someone's field and harvested wheat near Davenport, Washington. They'd bring their antique Oliver clectracs or horse-drawn harvesters from as far away as the Washington Peninsula and cut and sort the crop in the traditional way. Dust, sweat and axle grease defined those days. It felt good — a real, old-fashioned, backbreaking labor of love. They taught me how to honor the past and love the land. I bonded with them. The old boys sent me on another career path."

"What was that?"

"I got involved with the development and marketing of heirloom seeds."

"What's an heirloom seed?"

Shirley's eyes lit up as she launched into a mini-lecture of the difference between heirloom and hybrid seeds — those planted by agricultural combines for the mass production of crops. "We have original heirloom seeds from plants that date back to the 1600s."

"Cool," I nodded, still not comprehending the significance of her enthusiasm.

"I worked for the Victory Seed Company in Oregon and traveled to small farms across the northwest marketing these seeds to farmers who wanted to raise organic crops. Slow way to go at first, but the environmental movement took off in the 1980s, and I became a success."

"Good for you."

"The Northwest provides an incredible outdoor playground for adults. Close to the Pacific Ocean, the Olympics and the Cascades, I got into backpacking, kayaking, hiking and cross-country skiing. Then, a friend of mine started a travel group, and the entire world became an outdoor delight. We've traveled to exotic and far-off places like Tibet, China and Africa, pushed our physical limits and loved it."

"I'm very impressed with your accomplishments."

"When I retired in 2003, I bought Patricia Schultz's book, *1,000 Places to See Before You Die*. When I looked through it, I realized I had already been to and photographed more than two hundred of those locations. Since retirement, I have checked off another hundred places. The book appeals to my sense of curiosity. Now, I'm impatient and want to experience all I can while I'm robust and healthy."

The conversation ended with the arrival of our meals and both of us focused on satisfying our hunger and conversing with the other classmates who shared our table.

I admired Shirley's passion for travel and the way she embraced the mysteries of the natural world. As a youth, she seemed stifled, almost claustrophobic in school. Once she discovered the outdoors and the pursuit of all things natural, she blossomed into a healthy, vibrant person. *What a pleasant surprise,* I thought.

"They say the seeds of what we will do are in all of us, but it always seemed to me that in those who make jokes in life the seeds are covered with better soil and with a higher grade of manure."

— Ernest Hemingway

Chapter Twenty-Three: Celebrate, Celebrate, Dance to the Music

> "We dance for laughter, we dance for tears, we dance for madness, we dance for fears, we dance for hopes, we dance for screams, we are the dancers, we create the dreams."
> — Unknown

Near the end of dinner, the deep bass voice of Frank Montain, as emcee, interrupted table conversations and requested our attention.

Frank began the evening by recognizing members of the reunion committee, and the audience applauded the individuals for all their hard work. The committee had successfully located all but a handful of our classmates over the past two years. Then, in a theatrical fashion that only Frank could stage, he took off his glasses, lowered his voice and said in a serious tone, "I must also report that someone in this audience used our class website for personal gain. I know it's difficult to believe, but someone here actually went online to rekindle an old romance."

He paused for dramatic effect as people looked around the room, not knowing where Frank was going with this disclosure. "Since 1954, a shy young man had a crush on a girl who went to elementary school with him and also sat in several of his high school classes. The girl, raised in a traditional home, could not date boys and never knew of his hidden affection. Consequently, the young man never shared his feelings. After graduation they went separate ways, moved into adult life and lost track of each other."

Again, Frank put his glasses on and looked about the room. He let out a deep sigh, allowed a long moment to elapse and raised the index finger of his right hand. "But, fickle Cupid kept watching from a distance, waiting for the right moment. It came in the form of our website profile pages. At Christmas time this past year, the secret admirer saw his high school flame's profile and sent her a greeting. Their correspondence continued, followed by long distance phone calls, gifts and then visits. Cupid shot his arrows through cyberspace, and they hit their mark."

The audience laughed and then clapped as the details of the heartwarming story filled the room.

Frank put up his hands to signal for silence. He had more to say. "Then, after fifty years of wishing and wondering, the man asked his website connection to marry him. In August, one month ago, the couple, surrounded by family members, enjoyed a small "hippie" wedding ceremony. They are here tonight as living proof that love and happiness can happen at any time in life. Please greet Oak Ridge's newest "Cutest Alumni Couple" Jim and Anna Sibley!"

The room erupted with applause and laughter as Jim and Anna stood to acknowledge the moment.

Well, I'll be, I thought. *You can even find Machu Picchu on the Internet.*

I'll have to admit, the well-orchestrated program that followed filled our hearts with poignant moments — warm, humorous and sensitive. The reunion committee had done its homework and played to the sentimental needs of its audience.

Throughout the presentation, Frank shared several humorous stories from our past. Whenever he'd mention a particular event, participants giggled and pointed to the guilty individual who stood up and waved to the applause of our assembled group. Frank reminded us of the time someone covered the art teacher's watercolors with clear nail polish, making it impossible for her to demonstrate a painting technique. He dramatically took off his glasses, looked at the audience and said, "Okay, it's time to come clean ... which one of you did this dastardly deed?"

The audience looked from table to table until three men, fondly remembered as quiet class nerds, stood and claimed credit for the prank. Laughter followed because none of us ever imagined these choirboy characters had the guts or motivation to pull off such a prank. *You just never know about people*, I thought. *They can surprise you.*

A high-tech slide show followed Frank's storytelling and evoked lots of tears. The reunion committee located our kindergarten pictures and blended them into a montage on a CD disc. Slides that followed captured memories of our campus life, showing our enthusiastic, energetic faces, full of hope — reflecting an unburdened, simple time, when only having close friends and living in the moment mattered most.

Finally, the CD ended with photos of our senior pictures matched with current images, candid shots taken by roving photographers over the previous days and hours. When my image flashed across the screen, no boos could be heard in the room. *At least, I got past that hurdle,* I thought.

The CD, of course, became an instant crowd pleaser and offered participants a meaningful keepsake from the reunion. A few comical awards based on people's statements from the class website closed the program on a high note. When the lights came up, Frank invited us to stay, mingle and enjoy the open bar. He also added that the combo in the next room promised to play slow favorites from our era.

I purchased another Rusty Nail and walked around the room, sitting at various tables to chat with people I had previously talked with during the weekend. Now, however, I chose to be an observer and listener more than a talker because I didn't want to evoke additional confrontations. To my surprise, no one cared because they enjoyed being involved with their own lives. Realizing I had not been the center of their universe, I appreciated the anonymity. Nursing a second drink, I thought, *Perhaps Linda had been correct. People really don't hold a grudge for fifty years. Was it possible they have forgiven me? No, that's too easy.*

I passed a table and looked at a woman chatting with her husband. The elaborate, colorful tattoo entwined on her left arm helped me recognize Beth. I stopped and smiled at the couple. My presence made them look up at me. I nodded and smiled. Beth jumped out of her chair and threw her arms around me.

"Mark, I'm so glad you returned. It's been forever."

"I see you've turned my gift into a beautiful piece of body art," I commented, inspecting the tattoo on her arm.

"I got the original design on a tragic night, many years ago, but I have had so much fun turning it into an artistic gem," she smiled. Looking down at her husband, Beth introduced me as "Mark, the design specialist," and grinned.

"Beth, I want to apologize for what happened to you that night, but I guess you recovered nicely."

"Thanks, but I never hated you for anything that went down. I adopted the philosophy that sometimes terrible things happen to people, and you have to make the most of a bad situation."

I shook my head in disbelief. The accident, as it turned out, had not left traumatic scars on Beth. In fact, she turned her injury into a fashion statement. In that moment, another guilty weight from the past lifted from my heart.

"Just don't ever ask me to go race with you again."

"I won't. I promise," I said, crossing my fingers and flashing her a smile.

Beth turned away, sat down at the table and rejoined her husband. Just like that, my "confrontation" with Beth ended.

That old worry had vanished. It evaporated with her smile and an attractive tattoo. I felt relieved, lighthearted, and began searching the room for Carol's face.

I approached her table, and she looked at me. "How's it going for you, apology boy?"

"Surprisingly smooth. You were right about Beth. She's a very generous woman. I'm still looking for Terry. Have you seen him?"

"He's not here. They couldn't come. Someone told me a family emergency forced them to change plans."

"Too bad. ... I guess I'll have to send him a card from Sweden."

"That's not funny, mister."

"I know, but I couldn't resist."

Music drifting from the other room interrupted our talk and triggered my need to dance — the way I used to express my joy as a youth. I grabbed Carol by the hand and asked, "Would you please dance with your former boyfriend?"

"Sure."

I escorted Carol to the dance floor, feeling like a nervous teenager. We held each other and began to sway to a quiet two-step. To my surprise, people clapped, and two more couples joined us.

"My hands are sweating like we were still kids," I said.

Carol smiled and said, "That's why we all had to wear those white gloves back then."

"Not at our sock hops in the gym," I countered.

"Don't you remember those formal dance lessons at the Twentieth Century Dance Club?"

"Oh, yes. I recall how we all had to dress up in suits and dresses to learn how to waltz, fox trot and rumba." I laughed at the distant memory I tried to blot out of my past.

"I remember the dance teachers showing us where to place our hands to make sure we didn't soil each other's clothing."

"Me, too, … and with our raging hormones, all we wanted to do was get close, hold on and touch each other."

Carol laughed, "But, not during the dance lessons." She hit me on the shoulder, and it reminded me of Linda again. *Why do all the significant woman in my life feel the need to slug my arm?* I asked myself.

"You're right. It took a few more years and a cultural revolution to change things," I responded.

"Sometimes I feel sad about all the changes that took place in our lives after graduation," she added. "We were so naive and graduated from high school without any worries. I sort of miss those days."

"You can never go back in time, Carol," I began to philosophize. "We dance our dreams throughout our lives. Back then, we didn't know all of the steps and often were out of sync with the rhythm, but it was our dance — and we got up and moved about — improvised, felt the beat and danced with joy."

"That's a corny image, but I like it. In truth, that's what we did," she smiled.

"We may not have been the best dancers on the floor of life, but we invented a lot of new steps, changed the beat and forged a different world."

The music stopped, and I sensed a change in Carol's mood. "Are you ready for tomorrow?" she asked.

"I'm not sure how to begin. I hope I can figure it out before breakfast, Carol …," I hesitated and tried to find the next words.

"Yes?" she asked.

"What did you mean this afternoon when you said you'd never choose to hurt me?"

Carol looked away and didn't answer. Finally, she said, "Nothing, Mark. … It meant nothing."

I pursued her apparent reluctance, but she put her finger to her lips, signaling me not to say any more.

"It may have been difficult to talk with me this afternoon," Carol said, "but you did it and survived. We're in a much better place tonight. Don't worry about tomorrow ... just speak from your heart. Tell them what you remember, and it will be fine."

I gave her a quick hug and headed back to the bar for a night cap. I planned to leave the party early and get a good night's sleep. I wanted to be alert and refreshed for the meeting with Ed and Theresa. It would be a watershed moment in my life, and I needed to be ready for whatever occurred.

> "I know now that there is no one thing that is true — it is all true."
> — Ernest Hemingway

Chapter Twenty-Four: The Resolution

"Resolve and thou art free."
— Henry Wadsworth Longfellow

At 9:45 a.m., I heard a soft knock. Already showered and shaved, I had been awake for hours. I must have looked startled when I opened the door and saw Carol smiling at me. She had a pot of coffee and two cups on a tray.

"I thought you could use the support of an old friend," she smiled, transferring the treasured caffeine into my hands. She poured two steaming cups and handed one to me. I placed it on the table and gave Carol a long, warm hug, letting out a deep breath. She could sense my anxiety and held me in silence.

"Thank you, dear friend. I appreciate your sensitivity," I whispered as I wiped away an unexpected tear.

"Are you ready?" she asked.

"I've gone over every detail of what happened that night. And every time I say the words out loud, I realize how dumb we were playing around like that."

"Quit beating yourself up. You were a kid. ... We all felt invincible at that age."

"You're right. Of course, you're right, but that doesn't justify our actions. The disaster still happened … and it was my fault."

"We were all to blame," she said. "They need to hear your version of the story."

"I know. Will you be joining us for the meeting?"

"No, Mark," she said looking away. "This is your show, and I'd be in the way. You need to do this by yourself."

"Okay, but thanks for coming up … and the coffee. Nice way to tell me you care."

"You're welcome." She looked at her watch, gave me another quick hug and softly said, "It's time. I'll slip out the hotel's side door. Good luck, Mark. I'm totally confident you can do this." She left and disappeared down the hall.

I took a deep breath, exhaled slowly, looked at myself in the mirror and said out loud, "It's your time to be honest, Mark!"

The elevator dropped to the lobby, and it opened to both Ed and Theresa facing me. I greeted them with a handshake, and we walked to the hotel restaurant, nervously engaged in forced small talk about the weather. The waiter took our orders, poured coffee and left us alone.

"I'm really glad you accepted my invitation to breakfast this morning," I began. "This will probably be the most difficult conversation in my life."

They sat quietly and stared at me. Neither helped me get started.

"This talk is long overdue," I continued. "I need to share what happened that night with both of you."

"I didn't want to come here," snapped Theresa. "But your ex-girlfriend convinced me to give you some time. She said closure is important no matter how long it takes."

"As far as I'm concerned, Mark, I needed to hear, firsthand, how and why my brother died that night. I blamed you for his death and never understood how the police could let you go without charging you with manslaughter." Ed's eyes glared at me, adding a crimson glow to his face.

I looked at both of them and quietly offered an initial apology. "I know how both of you feel. I understand your anger. I take full responsibility for the game we played. For that I sincerely apologize. I hope someday you can find it in your hearts to forgive me. If you still blame me after I share my story, I'll understand."

They both stared at me with emotionless expressions. Neither offered a sign of compassion. *Speaking the truth must be part of the mea culpa process,* I thought. *I never fully understood the meaning of repentance in that junior high catechism class, but I didn't need to before today.*

"I have carried the guilt and remorse of that night with me for the past fifty years. I realize you can't run or hide from such a mistake, but I tried. Those things don't go away. Those memories have been a barrier to my life. When the reunion committee located me, I realized I had to do this now or die an unhappy man. I came back to apologize and find peace. So here I am, sitting in front of you, asking for your forgiveness."

The food arrived and, thankfully, broke the growing tension. *This isn't going well at all*, I thought. I stopped talking for a moment and let them prepare to eat breakfast. I couldn't eat. My appetite had vanished. I pushed my plate out of the way, so I could speak directly to both of them. Ed and Theresa began nibbling at their food, but kept looking at me. They studied my face and waited for me to say more. I took them back to that night.

It was three weeks before graduation on a hot, humid Saturday night, and Tim scored a couple of cases of beer from Buddy. We were feeling pretty good and looking for some action. The girls suggested we go play at the quarry, and we jumped into four cars for the short trip.

The cops had Harlem Avenue staked out, so that ended our drag racing. And since the warm weather had set in, they were also patrolling Thatcher Woods to break up any drinking or make-out parties. So, the quarry became a good choice.

I figured out how to get past the gate earlier in the year and invented a game to test our skills and courage. Quarry quest challenged us to see who could get the most out of his vehicle and still retain control.

We marked out two side-by-side tracks in the dirt — each approximately a hundred yards long. The raceway led from the middle of the service road to the edge of the quarry pit. The object of the game was to *reve* up the car's engine until it redlined at the maximum RPMs and then let out the clutch and race at top speed toward the edge of the quarry. At the last second, the driver who chickened out first, slammed on his brakes and stopped before going over the edge. We'd almost always end the run simultaneously. We weren't crazy. The closest car to the edge would be crowned 'quarry quest champion.' The champ got free lunches for the next week and all the beer he could drink.

It was so cool. The drag race and sudden stop created a rush more exciting than any pot Buddy could ever sell us. However, after a while, even quarry quest grew dull. So, we upped the stakes. Each driver carried passengers who wanted to experience the thrill. Then, we started playing the game at night … without headlights.

It was a typical Saturday night. We drank some beer, but we weren't drunk. Our radios were blasting, and the girls danced in the headlights. Then, Tim challenged me to a quarry quest. At that hour, we were tired and not thinking straight. I beat him the previous week, and he wanted a rematch. Stupidly, I accepted. We had raced at the quarry a hundred times. Both of us knew the track, knew our limits and felt in control.

Several people jumped in our two cars to experience the ultimate thrill. Carol rode shotgun next to me, Ruth Ann got in behind me, and Ryan sat next to her. Beth jumped in the front of Tim's car, and Terry sat in the back. They had never been on a quarry quest before that night and wanted to feel the rush.

Everything was cool. Friends cheered. Tim and I exchanged high signs, switched off our headlights and stepped on it. Tonight the road felt different, like we were driving through a bowl of chocolate pudding. However, I thought I could handle it, but we started fishtailing. Ruth Ann began screaming, and Ryan yelled 'stop, stop.' Ruth Ann's fingernails dug into my shoulder, and I remember reaching up to release her grip.

I turned on my lights and saw the panic in Tim's eyes. I could hear Beth's piercing scream coming from Tim's vehicle. We had overshot our marks, and I stomped on the brakes with both feet.

Then, for some unknown reason, my car veered off to the right and began to tumble sideways getting closer to the edge of the pit. Suddenly, we were airborne — flying into the quarry. Ruth Ann screamed, "No, No," and Ryan yelled, "We're going to die."

The last thing I remember was striking a huge rock outcropping on the way down and hitting my head on the windshield. I woke up in the hospital and a week later, they sent me home to heal.

I stopped talking and looked at Ed and Theresa. She couldn't restrain herself and showered me with a verbal outburst. "You stupid, idiotic kids. Didn't you think about the consequences, the danger?" She slammed down her coffee cup, spilling the brown liquid across the table. Both Ed and I jumped at her sudden move and the resulting flood of coffee headed toward our laps. A bus boy standing nearby came to the rescue and wiped away the dark river before any damage occurred.

I took a deep breath and said, "Of course, you're right, Theresa. We were foolish ... crazy, but no one dared back down.

"You mean you left your brains at home. You can't stop a three thousand pound car from going over the edge of a hundred foot cliff."

I took a deep breath, exhaled and looked into Ed's eyes. "Ed, I loved your brother. He was my best friend. I haven't found anybody who I've been closer to since we lost him. You've got to believe me. I would never hurt him on purpose. We were ...." I couldn't continue. I held my napkin to my face and wept. I cried from deep inside. I hadn't felt such agony since I realized what happened that night. Ed and Theresa waited for me to stop. They knew more explanation was necessary and neither felt satisfied with my story.

"I'll be right back," I said. I made my way to the bathroom to wash my face. *Hold on, Mark,* I told myself. *You're almost there. It will take a little more inner strength, but you have to finish.* "You can do this," I spoke into the mirror and wiped the water off my face. Temporarily refreshed, I returned to an audience whose eyes had been fixed on me from the moment I stepped out of the men's room.

To my surprise, I saw Carol sitting with Ed and Theresa. The waiter had already brought a cup and poured her coffee. Our eyes met and my lips formed a silent thank you. Carol ignored me and looked solemnly at the table.

Although I was puzzled by her presence, I continued my story.

"Now, fifty years later, I realize my memory of that night has a few missing pieces. I've gone over it in my head more than a thousand times and still can't figure out how the accident happened. I recall that the track was wet but it shouldn't have caused the car to roll and go airborne."

"Oh, my god," Theresa said. "It hurts just to think about it."

"I found out Tim was lucky. Instead of plunging into the pit below, his car slowly coasted down the embankment and got snagged on the limb of a dead tree sticking out of the hill. Tim held on for dear life. Terry, thrown free by the impact, landed safely on an outcropping of rocks and only broke his arm. The jolt caused Beth to shove her arm through the side window, and she cut it up pretty bad — needed surgery to repair the arteries. When the fire department arrived, Tim's car hung on the branch like a battered Christmas ornament."

"Police told me that my car rolled sideways over the edge and into the quarry, hitting several rock outcroppings along the way. When the car bounced and launched into empty space, it plunged to the bottom of the pit. Ryan and Ruth Ann died when they were ejected from the back seat. By the time we reached the bottom, the car landed with such force that I flew through the front windshield. The glass cut my head and injured my windpipe. Carol broke her tailbone."

I stopped to breathe again and ran my fingers across my fifty-year-old scars. The uncomfortable silence ended when Carol gasped, whimpered and covered her face with the napkin. Surprised by her reaction, the three of us looked at her and failed to understand.

She allowed the napkin to drop and said, "Mark may not be able to remember the details, but there is something all of you need to know." Carol paused to take a breath. "I'm the one who really caused the accident. I'm the one who is responsible for killing Ruth Ann and Ryan, not Mark."

Carol grabbed her napkin again and wept with mournful sobs into its folds. I sat back in my chair and stared at her. Her words did not make sense. A rush of questions filled my mind and begged for answers. Ed and Theresa looked as stunned as I did. We waited until Carol could speak.

Wiping away streaked mascara and tears, she blew her nose in the cloth napkin and gasped for air.

Her eyes, already red and puffy, created a desperate look, yet she forced out more words. "Everyone thinks Mark caused the accident, but it was my fault."

"What!" I said.

Ed and Theresa looked on in disbelief. Another flood of tears caused her to hide her face in the napkin again. Customers at the other tables stared in our direction, and the conscientious waiter hovered nearby in case we needed his assistance. I waved him off, and my look let other guests know the matter was none of their concern. Between soft moans and sound of uneven breathing, she finally regained enough control to look up at us.

She wiped her nose again and continued. "I reacted like a jealous high school girl."

"None of this makes sense," Theresa said.

"I'll explain ... Mark," she said, looking into my eyes, "I thought you were cheating on me.

As soon as I got in the front seat next to you, I knew there was something going on between you and Ruth Ann. I looked at her sitting behind you ... smiling, and ... and ... she had the audacity to play with the hair on the back of your neck. Don't you remember?"

I sat with my mouth open and shook my head. "I went out with Ruth Ann the previous weekend, but I didn't love her. I couldn't remember anything about her touching my hair, just her fingernails buried in my shoulder."

"I watched the way she looked at you. She sat behind you so she could touch you ... rub your back. Ruth Ann didn't think I could see her in the dark, but I did."

"Carol, we were just kids. Flirting and horsing around was a part of the whole dating thing."

"I saw you reach for her hand, and I got angry. I wanted you to stop doing that in front of me, so I grabbed the steering wheel and jerked it to the right as hard as I could."

"Her nails hurt. They were digging into my shoulder, Carol, that's all."

"I'm so sorry. I never dreamed we'd wind up at the bottom of the quarry, killing two friends." Carol cried into her napkin, and the three of us let her sob.

"So, that's what made us tumble over the edge?" I said. "That's the missing piece I couldn't figure out."

"Oh, my god, I didn't know any of that ... nobody did." Ed spoke in a soft tone, almost as if this new revelation had slapped him.

"The worst part is that Ruth Ann didn't even like Ryan," Theresa mumbled. "She went out with him that night to try to make you jealous, Mark. She begged me to take her babysitting job so she could be with the group. If I had only refused, my sister would be alive today." Theresa started crying.

All talking ceased, and each of us drifted into our own thoughts about that night. An astute waiter left us alone even though the obligatory coffee service required his attention. After what seemed like an eternity, I looked around and signaled for the check. The waiter brought it to me and asked if I wanted a carryout box.

"No, thanks," I responded. "It's eleven, and the bar just opened. I think we all could use a stiff drink. Cold eggs won't do."

> "About morals, I know only that
> what is moral is what you feel good after
> and what is immoral
> is what you feel bad after."
> — Ernest Hemingway

Chapter Twenty-Five: Zoned Out

> "Home ... hard to know what it is
> if you've never had one
> Home ... I can't say where it is
> but I know I'm going home.
> That's where the heart is."
>
> — U2 lyrics

We sat sipping drinks without tasting anything. Lost in thought, we ignored the bar's ambiance: a warm Sunday in late September; the Chicago Bears battling the Philadelphia Eagles on television; classmates at a corner table, still celebrating the reunion; and the dutiful bartender drying and racking wine glasses. Emotionally zoned out, I only heard Ed and Theresa's labored breathing and Carol's soft crying.

Theresa spoke first. "Such idiots. Your foolish behavior cost Ryan and Ruth Ann their lives. It was stupid ... so unnecessary." She shook her head, drained her glass and ordered another drink.

Ed followed. "I looked up to my brother ... always wanted to be like him. That night, I lost my best friend. The accident turned my parents into overly protective hawks. It took years for them to trust me ... to feel safe whenever I left the house. I never became a normal teenager." He consumed the last of his beverage and blankly stared into the bottom of the empty glass.

"Life changed for me, as well," I said. "I shamed my family name, ran away, turned my back on Carol, and I've had to live with this unresolved issue for fifty years.

I could have gone to jail for involuntary manslaughter, but thanks to our small town culture, my parent's connections with the police and our family lawyer, we secured a good plea bargain. Juvenile court downgraded the charges from involuntary manslaughter to careless driving resulting in death.

They suspended my license for two years. Ironically, in all that time, I never needed to drive anywhere. Most people in Oak Ridge treated me like a criminal — thought I was a murderer. I couldn't handle it and had to leave."

"And I had to live here with a lie and my own private guilt for just as long," Carol said. "Life in Oak Ridge became a bitter reminder of my remorse every time I saw Ed or Theresa."

"And I roamed the world, thinking I was responsible for the deaths of my two friends."

"Now it's my turn to beg your forgiveness, Mark, Ed, Theresa. … Can you ever pardon me for what I did that night?"

Theresa patted her arm — an initial sign of human connection, but neither she nor Ed spoke words of compassion. They recognized our haunting pain, but were unwilling to console us.

"I'm glad I came back to the reunion," I said, "back to a home where the hurt is. I needed to feel this intensity. Perhaps this new disclosure can help us all finally find peace."

"Mark, I have directed my angry against you for much too long. Hearing your story has helped," Theresa said. "Carol, I have no idea how to process what you shared, but I'll try to forgive both of you in time."

"You know," Ed added, "in many ways, life took a dramatic turn for me without Ryan. I became an only child, and my parents spoiled me throughout high school. They went overboard to compensate for Ryan's death. I'll always miss Ryan, but his death put a different twist on my life."

"How's that, Ed?"

"As a teenager, I learned to live with pain and loss. For a long time that was confusing. I felt pressured to live up to expectations once reserved for Ryan. If my brother had lived, I wouldn't have had to shoulder his legacy, to perform, to please my parents, to live up to his memory. I know that sounds selfish, but in a way, a part of me died with him."

I let Ed dwell on his thoughts. Then he added, "I'm not sure how I feel about this chat. Nothing has changed. In fact, Carol's information has complicated things. But, thank you both for having the guts to step up and talk with us."

Carol and I dropped our heads and sat in our discomfort.

"It must have been torture to carry that information around for so long," Ed added. "In a way, I feel sorry for you two. You have lived your entire lives stuck in your own hell."

Suddenly, there was nothing more to say. We had nothing else in common. In an awkward move, we simultaneously finished our drinks, exchanged quick, unemotional looks, and Ed escorted Theresa out of the bar. Neither of them glanced back at us.

Carol looked stunned, and I felt exhausted. The confession left us both drained.

"We need to talk, but not now," I said. "I need some sleep. How about coming back here for dinner tonight?"

Carol silently agreed.

"Let's meet here around seven. I'm sure you need to rest as much as I do."

> "The best ammunition against lies is the truth, there is no ammunition against gossip. It is like a fog and the clear wind blows it away and the sun burns it off."
>
> — Ernest Hemingway

Chapter Twenty-Six: Starting Over

"The beginnings and endings
of all human undertakings are untidy."
— John Galsworthy

Just after 7 p.m., I came downstairs and spotted Carol sipping a glass of chardonnay. She looked both attractive and sad at the same time. She watched me cross the room. As I got closer, I saw her eyes glistening with fresh tears. She said nothing and didn't need to … her slumped shoulders and loosely brushed hair betrayed her emotions.

"Do you want to talk about what happened this morning?" she asked.

"In a minute. Let me order a drink first."

We sat quietly until the waiter brought Carol another glass of wine and me a Rusty Nail. Anxious to begin, Carol said, "I'm sorry if I blindsided you at breakfast. It would have been better … kinder … to have shared that truth with you when we were alone."

"True," I said. "But, I still don't remember any of those last-minute actions in the car. All I know is that it didn't turn out the way it should have."

"I decided to tell all of you at breakfast when I saw the tears in your eyes and sensed your confusion this morning. It wasn't fair, and I could no longer keep my secret."

"Carol, I want you to know that I loved you and only flirted with other girls. I never knew your feelings about me were so intense."

"As a teenager, Mark, saying 'I love you' was so difficult for you. I never knew how you felt about me."

"It still is difficult. So, in our own way, we were both responsible for what happened and paid a lifelong penalty for our juvenile behavior," I said.

"Outwardly, you suffered for it more than me," she said.

"Yes, I did."

"How have you been treated at the reunion?"

"I'd say this trip has turned out to be the most frightening, courageous and daring experience I've ever had — another life changing event."

"Me, too. Once you called, I knew I had to find a way to share the truth with all of you."

"How sad. It could have been resolved years ago."

"Mark, it took me almost a year after you left to want to explain my part in the accident. By that time, your parents had moved to Florida, and nobody knew how to get in touch with you."

"I know. I felt too guilty and angry with the people in Oak Ridge to ever think of coming back. I wanted to move on. That choice made me abandon you as well."

"The worst part," Carol said, "was not being able to say anything. I hid reality. My secret paralyzed me — tied me to an unpleasant past."

"Such a loss," I said. "We hid in our own shadows, preventing either of us from enjoying a full life."

"We were frightened kids who didn't know how to handle such a crisis and let circumstance control us."

Carol and I embraced as the tears flowed. Nothing more needed to be said. We had come to an understanding that surpassed words. We ordered dinner and engaged in superficial talk during the meal. Finally, over coffee, I returned to our relationship.

"You said something yesterday that had resonated in my brain for the past twenty-four hours."

"What's that?"

"Remember, you touched my face and said, 'What could have been.' "

"Oh, yes, I'm sorry if that bothered you. It was a temporary flight into my memory."

"No need to apologize. It started me thinking about the choices we make in life and, more importantly, the choices we *don't* make."

"What do you mean by the choices we *don't* make?"

"This weekend's experience reminded me of a film called *The Family Man*."

"I don't remember it," Carol said. "What's it about?"

"Nicolas Cage plays the main character. Early in life, Cage chooses the path to wealth rather than marriage to his college sweetheart, and they separate. He becomes a major player on Wall Street and lives quite well, but alone."

"Is this the Mark Pierce story?" she teased.

"Not even close," I said and continued. "After a life-threatening encounter, Cage wakes up in the morning in a different place and time — in some parallel universe where he's married to his college sweetheart, has a family and struggles with the usual financial issues and job security associated with a middle-class life. Cage experiences how life *would have been different* if he had chosen love instead of money."

"How does the movie turn out?"

"Rest assured, it's an American ending, but, the plot suggests that the choices one *doesn't make* may be as important as the one actually makes. Some people believe the road not taken is acted out in a parallel universe."

"Life in a parallel universe ... what life could have been for us if we had shared the truth back then, admitted our mistakes and followed our dreams."

"But we didn't, and circumstances sent us in a different direction. I regret that choice, but we found a different kind of happiness in other pursuits."

"Happiness seems to be an illusion and it can bloom wherever you choose to be," Carol said. "You can create happiness any time you want it."

"Even the idea of time is an illusion. Here we are ... two former high school sweethearts enjoying dinner ... fifty years later. By itself, it's a remarkable event, highly improbable of ever occurring. It's like time folded in on itself ... if only for this brief moment."

"That's why they schedule high school reunions, stupid. People can share their past, make new decisions and assess the value of their old choices."

I smiled at her insight and said, "And, *stupid me*, chose to miss all of those opportunities."

"The best part about *this* time warp," she grinned, "is that I'm no longer angry with you, and the truth has cleared up everything. Now we can start over."

"Does that mean you want to start dating again?" I asked.

She laughed aloud and smacked me on the shoulder. "No, you've got a wonderful woman in San Francisco that loves you, and I've got my life here. Let's just remain friends."

"Good," I responded with a smile, "Linda warmed me about hitting on old girlfriends."

We both chuckled. Another hour passed, and we finished dinner. Carol and I exchanged e-mail addresses and phone numbers. Carol promised to call when she came to San Francisco to meet Linda and renew our friendship. *Nice intent, but it probably won't happen,* I thought.

The first thing she planned to do in the morning was to report her part in causing the accident to the police to see if there were any repercussions for what happened in 1961. I assured her that nothing would come of it.

The night ended, and I headed back to the hotel. I went upstairs to pack and prepare to catch my morning flight to San Francisco. I set out my notebook, so I could jot down a few thoughts on the flight home.

> "Maybe ... you'll fall in love
> with me all over again."
> "Hell," I said, "I love you enough now.
> What do you want to do? Ruin me?"
> "Yes. I want to ruin you."
> "Good," I said. "That's what I want too."
> — Ernest Hemingway

Chapter Twenty-Seven:
The Flight Back to Reality

"A memory is what is left when something happens and does not completely unhappen."
— Edward de Bono

At thirty-five thousand feet, my mind danced with reflections of my four-day experience in Oak Ridge. I had come to the reunion on a quest and discovered the answers to the nagging questions I had about my past. In the process, I apologized to former friends and my high school sweetheart. In turn, her confession released me from years of self-imposed guilt and regret. The classmates I met freed me from the gnawing fear that I started life by making the wrong decision.

I looked out the window at the harvested fields of Iowa below and opened the notebook to record my thoughts.

> *It took fifty years to muster enough courage to apologize. Waiting such a long time created havoc in my life. How strange for a human to postpone a difficult task out of fear?*

I took a deep breath and added,

> *I'm upset with myself for taking so long to grow up and face reality. I spent so much time suppressing my fears that the energy it took to do so got in the way of enjoying my life. I regret that now.*

The flight attendant asked me for my drink order and interrupted my thoughts. After munching the tiny bag of pretzels and downing the last of the ginger ale, I returned to my notebook.

> *Dwelling on "what could have been" is the real-life definition for unproductive thinking. You only end up with disappointment. Any decision made in the past supports your best thinking at the time you made it. You have to accept the consequences that follow. Funny, life works that way.*

I reflected on Father's McCray's insights about the fear of change and penned,

> *Regardless of the ordinary fears people feel, real or imagined, most of my classmates seem happy. Some remained in the comfort zone of Oak Ridge, relying on familiar patterns, family and friends for support and consistency. The others, who chose to explore places outside of their comfort zone, seemed just as happy. We all deal with whatever life brings and live with it.*

I put down my pen and examined the drawing that Joseph and I created at the hotel bar. I wrote: *People choose to leave their comfort zone to find a mystical Machu Picchu ... to fulfill their dreams. What does Machu Picchu represent?*

- *Pursuing adventure*
- *Following a spouse or partner*

- *Giving self or service to others*
- *Grasping at the joys of life with tenacity*
- *Finding intellectual challenges*
- *Listening to the voice of God*
- *Hearing the call of the wild beg for your presence*
- *Searching for wealth*
- *Following the encouragement of a mentor*
- *Discovering an untapped skill*

I set my pen aside again and admired my detective work. I smiled at the image of Joy publicly displaying trophies of uncommon wealth and Buddy's transformation from a school bully. I opened another page and wrote:

How do you define happiness?
It didn't matter if people stayed in Oak Ridge or pursued a self-directed odyssey. Happiness is defined and measured by one's own criteria — a personal perception of bliss. Reunions, like this, offer people capstone experiences to celebrate the choices we made. Is it better to live in or out of the zone? Take your pick. They both work. The important thing is to celebrate the life we chose.

I closed the notebook and then my eyes. My mind operated on overload, and I had to turn it off. I slept until the pilot's voice announced our initial descent into San Francisco.

Walking past security, I spotted Linda's smiling face. From a distance, I marveled at her beauty, as a flood of memories from our ten-year romance raced through my mind. We embraced with a lingering hug, followed by a deep kiss. Her body felt warm and inviting. *Strange, I left Oak Ridge and kept running until I discovered my comfort zone with Linda, the keeper of our own Inca sanctuary.* That realization pleased me.

"Um," she whispered, "that's a nice greeting. You need to go away alone more often, so we can have this kind of homecoming. How was the trip?"

"Thank you for insisting I go back. I have so many things to share."

"Then, tell me all about it as we head home."

"Worry a little bit every day and in a lifetime you will lose a couple of years. If something is wrong, fix it if you can. But train yourself not to worry: Worry never fixes anything."
— Ernest Hemingway

A final thought about making life choices …

From *Return to Love* by Marianne Williamson

"Our deepest fear is not that we are inadequate. Our deepest fear is that we are powerful beyond measure. It is our light, not our darkness, that most frightens us. We ask ourselves, who am I to be brilliant, gorgeous, talented, and fabulous? Actually, who are you not to be? You are a child of God. Your playing small doesn't serve the world. There's nothing enlightened about shrinking so that other people won't feel insecure around you. We are all meant to shine, as children do. We are born to make manifest the glory of God that is within us. It's not just in some of us, it's in everyone. And as we let our own light shine, we unconsciously give other people permission to do the same. As we are liberated from our own fear, our presence automatically liberates others."

(p.165, hardback)

About the Author

Bill Lamperes graduated from Oak Park-River Forest in 1961. The son of Greek and German parents with a limited education, Bill became the only one in his family to go to college. His brother inherited his father's barbershop, and his sister married young and raised a family.

After graduating from Northern Illinois University with a B.A. in history and a teaching certificate, Bill began his extensive educational career as a sixth grade teacher in St. Charles, Illinois, then moved to Colorado in 1969 where he taught in the Poudre School District in Fort Collins, Colorado, for the next thirty years.

Bill earned his Master's degree from Northern Illinois University in 1972 and completed his Doctorate at Carnegie-Mellon University in Pittsburgh, Pennsylvania, in 1985. After serving as a one-year-only principal of an alternative high school, an assignment that lasted twelve years, Bill published his first book, *Making Change Happen: Shared Vision, No Limits*. The publication sent him to Arizona for another five years to create and run another alternative high school.

Bill retired in 2008 to pursue his passion to write fiction novels and stories. *Out of the Zone* is a tribute to his classmates from Oak Park-River Forest High School. Bill can be reached via his website: www.blamperesauthor.com

Books by the Author

Non-Fiction Book:

Making Change Happen: Shared Vision, No Limits. Lanham, Maryland: Scarecrow Education 2005. The story explains how a group of educators redesigned an alternative high school and turned it into a national education model. The book outlines more than one hundred strategies the staff used to modify its program, motivate students to succeed and garner support from the community and district administrators.

Fiction Books:

Bar Exam: Tavern Tales and Reflections. Bloomington, Indiana: iUniverse, 2009. The book presents a fascinating dialogue between ordinary regulars who frequent The Benbow Inn, a hotel tucked along the Eel River in Northern California. Their discussions range from the meaning of life to how to make love last. Their stories filled with humor, sadness and hope speak to the desire in all of us to make a difference and live a fulfilled life.

Depositions, Bloomington, Indiana, iUniverse, 2009. A prominent citizen of a small Illinois community dies in a one-car accident. It's routine to the police until they discover the victim, dressed in a three-piece suit, is wearing his bedroom slippers. The twisting tale of suspense and mystery creates trouble for a nosey writer looking for an idea for his next novel. Co-authored with the spirit of Leon Palles, a man who died in 1996, the novel is adapted from Leon's original screenplay.

The Attendant, Bloomington, Indiana, iUniverse, 2010. The Attendant was originally posted on the Internet as an April fool's joke by the Bristol Evening Report in London, England. The book transitioned into a novel when the author decided to create a story that gave life to the daring parking lot attendant who thought he successfully scammed the system.

Out of the Zone, Create Space.com. A novella dedicated to my high school classmates for our reunion, scheduled in September, 2011. Out of the Zone is the story of a man who returns to his high school reunion in order to resolve past sins. He left town immediately after graduation because he committed an act that turned his entire class against him. He wants to apologize for his actions and seek forgiveness before he dies.

Voices, currently being edited, will be published in early 2012. *Voices* tells the story of a writer whose wife is killed in a tragic hit-and-run accident. In his quest to find justice, the writer hears the voices of ghosts, spirits and the living who give him clues to help solve the crime.

Made in the USA
Charleston, SC
26 May 2011